A Deadly Couple

Mark Sanders

Chapter 1

Saturday January 1st, New Year's Day

Grace Canning opened her eyes with the slow motion of someone preparing herself for the pain that would doubtless follow. Sure enough, the pain of the expected hangover from last night's New Year's Eve party started almost immediately. First, the pounding began. Then the room started to spin. First one way, then, as she rose from her bed and ran towards the bathroom, the other. The contents of her last meal plus several martini cocktails were quickly expelled into the toilet basin.

As Grace heaved and threw up the last of the contents of her now empty stomach, she made the first of her new year resolutions that she would undoubtedly break within the first month of this new year.

'Definitely, no more alcohol for Moi', she whispered to herself in a mock French accent before climbing back into bed and pulling up the sheets until she was once again completely covered, fuzzy thoughts of the night before still swirling around her head.

At Thirty-five years old, Grace Canning had a decent job, lived in a decent apartment, in a decent neighbourhood. She lived a decent life, had a decent car, and was not short of money. What she didn't have in abundance were friends, and in particular, boyfriends.

Grace was lonely.

Whilst everyone arrived at the office party with their partners last night, Grace waited patiently at 'Arnolds' bar. She waited for over an hour, feeling more like a prostitute looking for clients than someone who had resorted to the internet to find love. Eventually, there was a telling 'ping' on her mobile phone. Reading the short but very sharp message Grace had a tear in her eye.

'Sorry Grace. Can't make it tonight. Better offer!'.

'You bastard!', she yelled at the phone and for a brief moment thought seriously about throwing the piece of tech across the bar. She was stopped in her tracks by the not so young woman behind the bar.

'Don't do it love. He's not worth it. Drink this'.

'What?'.

The older woman leaned across and handed Grace the glass she had been preparing for another customer.

'On the house. A dry martini, shaken not stirred. Just like James Bond has it'.

Grace took the drink and drank it down in one.

'Better?', asked the bar tender.

Nodding, Grace managed a 'Yeah, thanks', before heading out the door and off to the party.

There was a light dusting of snow on the ground as Grace finally pulled back the curtains bringing the slightest of smiles to her otherwise saddened face. She loved the snow, had been an accomplished skier in her youth back in the day but it had been a while since her last outing on ski's. Maybe this year she'd get back out onto the slopes, somewhere. Not here, not London.

Stretching in front of her fourth-floor apartment window she noticed a couple walking hand in hand along the sidewalk down below. They were in love. They had to be. It was evident in their body language. His hand went from hers to wrap around a slender waist bringing her in closer. Laughter too. As they walked, he made her laugh with a whisper in her ear.

What had he said to make her laugh so? A promise of something yet to come. A reminder of an event the night before?

Grace trudged back over to her bed and pulled up the sheets once more, remembering her own disastrous New Year's Eve. An office party, full of middle-aged men, desperate middle-aged men, with their middle-aged partners, and her. What a disaster it was.

The sun was glistening off the snow-covered street when Grace finally awoke for the third time that day. Drinking two glasses of water, along with two aspirin, she quickly dressed. Retrieving the unwanted diary, she turned to today's date and wrote in capitals:

'NEW JOB, NEW MAN, NEW ADVENTURE'

Grace Canning picked up her keys and started to run.

Chapter 2

Tom Ford stood facing across the street at the old Victorian building on Tavistock Place. The offices of Miles, Mackenzie Partners were located on the top floor of the imposing building and sat atop several other firms of London Accountants. Dressed in a charcoal grey suit, black leather brogues, accompanying black leather gloves, and three-quarter length wool overcoat Tom Ford entered the boardroom and sat before the three-man interview panel looking the businessman his CV outlined him to be.

An hour later he shook hands with the formidable looking Charles Perkins, the Head Partner of the one hundred- and ten-year-old firm in the old man's office.

'Welcome aboard Tom. It was a unanimous decision from all three Partners'.

'Thank you, Mr Perkins'.

'Charles, please'.

'Thank you, Charles'.

'Let me show you to your office. There's no name plate on the door yet but we can fix that this week'.

'Don't worry Charles. Being a little anonymous can sometimes work in your favour', replied Tom with a smile.

Charles Perkins opened the door and invited Tom to leave first. Accepting the invite Tom walked purposefully through the door straight into the bosom of a young woman stood outside the door.

Tom had nowhere else to go and managed to catch the woman before she fell backwards. However, the envelope she had been holding and which she had clearly been about to deliver to Mr Perkins dropped to the floor.

'Ooops. I'm terribly sorry Miss. Let me get that for you', exclaimed Tom. The young woman started to protest that it was not necessary, but Tom already had the envelope in his hand and was offering it back to the now red-faced female.

Grace had been thinking and then rethinking her decision.

Since that disastrous New Year, she had told herself that this year was going to be different. Grace was going to take her life somewhere else. Resignation letter in hand, she stood for the briefest of moments outside Mr Perkins office just allowing her beating heart to return to some level of normality. Once she knocked the door in front of her there was no going back. It was still early and most of the staff had yet to arrive. It was now or never.

'Ok Gracie. Here goes nothing'.

Grace raised her right hand, closed her eyes, and went for it. Expecting a contact with the impressive mahogany wood door her attempt at a knock met with only fresh air causing her to stumble and fall forward.

The reality of the situation literally hit Grace full on. Just as her hand prepared to knock the door itself swung open and Grace was propelled into the arms of a handsome stranger being shown out by Mr Perkins himself. Grace was so shocked she dropped her resignation letter and seemed to be in something of a daze. The stranger apologised, although she couldn't actually hear the words so mesmerised was she by this beautiful man before her. She could feel herself reddening up and becoming flushed in the face.

'Sorry', replied the beautiful stranger.

'Why?', replied Grace, staring at him a little too intensely.

Tom Ford was stood in the doorway not sure what to do next. This attractive woman stood in front of him seemed to have an issue with him and there was something of an impasse. He noted the letter was sealed and addressed to his new boss Mr Perkins. She was clearly an employee, aesthetically pleasing, but obviously not at ease here. He decided to go again with another apology and his best smile.

'I'm sorry. Shall I….'.

It was also a question relating to the letter he still held, and which was addressed to Mr Perkins who broke the brief and strange silence with his own introduction.

'Ah, Miss Canning. This is Mr Ford our new Business Support Manager and your new boss'.

Grace was still a little overwhelmed at the sight before her as the handsome stranger further responded with, 'Pleased to meet you, Miss Canning. Did you want this….'.

This was a year for making decisions Grace had told herself the previous evening and sometimes those decisions need to be made on the move. Quickly, impulsive. This was the time to make such a decision.

Snatching the envelope from his hand Grace managed a brief response.

'Oh good, I'll like that', acknowledging Mr Perkins introduction, before turning and marching off towards her desk in the distance leaving both men a touch confused and exasperated.

'Don't worry Tom, you'll get used to her'.

'Oh, I'm not worried', replied Tom, deep in thought.

Chapter 3

By the time Grace had returned to her desk she was hyperventilating so much she had to sit down and compose herself for a few moments.

'What is wrong with you Gracie? Pull yourself together', she scolded herself.

Just as her cheeks had returned to a less flushed colour and her heart had slowed to its normal pace, it started racing once more when a knock at the door was quickly followed by that face again. Her new boss had popped his head around the door.

'Mr Ford. I erm…can I help you with something?'.

'Yes. And the name is Tom'.

'Whose name is Tom?', asked Grace, her face reddening up once more.

'Mine'.

'Oh, right'.

Grace noticed he was holding two take-away cartons of something, and one was being thrust in her direction.

'What's that Mr Ford?'.

'It's Tom and this is a cup of really hot coffee. If you don't take it soon it's going to burn my hands'.

Grace quickly grabbed the coffee carton and placed it on her desk. It was really hot. How is he still holding his she thought to herself?

Tom pulled up a chair and sat opposite Grace taking a sip of his coffee. Grace, who was still stood as if expecting to be told to sit like a pupil in front of the principal, was silent.

'It's really good', said Tom.

'Sorry'.

'The coffee Grace. Do you mind if I call you Grace? I don't do formalities unless I really have to. I'm hoping we can be on first name terms as we are going to see a lot of each other'.

'Sure', replied Grace, her voice breaking.

Tom took another sip of his coffee as Grace squeaked her reply. He used his hand to indicate she should sit down. Tom knew she was nervous and intended to use this situation to his advantage. It was a great opportunity, and he was going to make the most of it. He was about to take a gamble but felt sure it would pay off.

'Am I making you nervous Grace?', asked Tom putting on his most infectious smile.

'A little. I guess'.

Leaning in closer and looking into her eyes he whispered.

'Grace, I need your help. I'm new here, have little experience in this type of work, and feel I may have made a mistake. I don't even know where my office is, or how anything works'.

Tom was only a couple of inches away from Grace's face. He noticed her hazel eyes were intently staring back into his. Her oval shaped pale face had a smattering of freckles around her nose and there were at least two piercings on each lobe. Her hair, a natural auburn colour had been dyed in the distant past. There was still evidence of colour on the tips of her shoulder length straight style. A simple gold neck chain bearing a plain cross hung loosely around the neck and dropped down towards her ample cleavage covered by a mustard-coloured silk blouse unbuttoned in a modest fashion. He noticed all these things within a few short seconds. It was what he did. It came natural to Tom.

At 36 years old Tom Ford was a formidable looking man. Six foot two inches tall, one hundred and ninety pounds, he was handsome, had professionally cut short light brown hair, and he wore his suit like a male model. He could turn his hand to just about anything. Having landed the role of Business Support Manager at one of London's most prestigious and oldest firms of accountants, a role he had never performed before, he was in need of acquiring the necessary tools to undertake the role, at least for a while until it was time to move on once more.

Grace Canning was going to be one of those tools.

Chapter 4

Grace was taken aback by Tom's request. But how could she refuse. She was almost melting in front of this man, inches away from her face. Was he about to kiss her? Should she reach in just a little more and take the plunge?

In an almost startled manner she pushed herself back, picked up the carton of coffee and took a long drink. It was still hot, and Grace's eyes grew wide.

Tom smiled at her as she rose.

'Hot?', he asked.

Grace nodded vigorously.

'I told you it was hot Grace'.

Standing whilst nodding, she couldn't talk but beckoned him to follow her towards the door a few paces behind her desk. There was no name plate but as she opened the door and invited Tom to walk through, he realised that this was his office. Smiling now, Tom couldn't believe his luck. The office itself was spacious with bookshelves lining the whole of the wall behind an exquisite mahogany desk. Tom wondered whether the firm had a job lot of mahogany desks. It was very much like the one in Mr Perkins office and a larger version of Grace's own. A small sofa was set below the full-length glass windows that gave him a view over the small green area opposite Tavistock Place. A leather armchair opposite the sofa and a small coffee table completed the inventory of office furniture.

The desk itself was sparse and held only a digital telephone system and a laptop computer.

As he surveyed his new workspace Grace walked over and stood in front of the windows. The light that shone in cast beams through the young woman's unlined skirt which gave Tom a silhouetted view of her figure from the waist down. It was a pleasing sight and Tom let himself linger at the view.

'It's a great view from here', he said, smiling at Grace.

Turning around to look out at the Central London scene she nodded before asking, 'Where would you like me first Tom?'.

Realising the unplanned innuendo in her question she quickly added, 'I mean what can I do for you first thing in the morning?'.

She was getting all flushed again and started to add something else but was interrupted by Tom's laughter stopping her in her tracks.

'Grace. We are going to get along great. I know it. Let's start with this laptop. If you can go through the office IT systems with me and any client lists I need to be aware of, that would be a great start'.

And for the next three hours Grace went through everything she knew about the office, and it's set up. The IT, telephone system, client lists, Tom's predecessor, the senior management team, and her own role within the machine. They only brought an end to their cosy training session when Mr Perkins knocked then walked in on them requesting Tom attend a business lunch with several potential new clients.

Tom nodded, put on his suit jacket, picked up his briefcase and headed towards the door. Just as he was about to close the door, he pooped his head back around.

'Thank you, Grace. I really appreciate your help'.

Grace smiled at her handsome new boss but before she could reply he had closed the door and was gone.

For the rest of the day Grace was distracted by her new boss. Not that he was anywhere to be seen. Grace never saw Tom for the rest of the day and at 5.30 pm she headed out the door and started walking towards Euston underground station not even noticing the light rain cascading down upon her uncovered head. Passers-by would probably question why this young woman was carrying an umbrella in the rain without any attempt to use it, even when the rain started to become even heavier. But for Grace, she didn't notice. Today had been a good day and nothing was going to ruin it.

The tube ride home did its best to spoil the day and took over forty five minutes even though it was only a half dozen stops. Something must have happened. Grace hated being in a crush and tonight it was not just a crush but a crush whilst stood still underground in between stops. After ten minutes people were becoming agitated. After twenty minutes they were ready to start banging on the driver's door. An announcement over the tube speaker system went some way to explaining the delay.

'Ladies and gentlemen. This is the driver speaking. Apologies for this unexpected delay but we are unable to proceed further at this time due to a Police incident. We hope to be moving forward shortly. Thank you'.

There were a number of groans from passengers plus a load more expletives aimed at the Police. Grace decided to keep her head down and wait it out.

Five minutes later the train moved, but at an alarmingly slow pace, until it crept into Archway underground station. There was only one more stop for her, but Grace decided against risking a further delay and alighted the train, preferring the walk the last half mile.

Grace eventually arrived at Flat 127d, Wood Lane, Highgate shortly after 7pm. She would normally expect to arrive home after work a good hour earlier, but these things happen. It had still been a good day overall. Pouring herself a large glass of Merlot, Grace Canning toasted herself.

'The future. I can do this'.

Kicking off her heels she sat on the sofa and reached for her diary. Carefully putting her glass down on the carpet Grace flipped the pages until she arrived at Tuesday the 4th January where she wrote just a few words.

'I think I've just met my future husband'.

Chapter 5

Tom acquitted himself very favourably at the lunchtime meeting. His photographic memory helped massively, and Mr Perkins was impressed by his knowledge of the firm's client base. The fact that the meeting was attended by three other potential clients, all of whom were middle aged women, also helped his cause. Within minutes of sitting down at the restaurant table Tom had all three ladies' attention with his knowledge of Italian food and more importantly, the Italian language, ordering for everyone in the mother tongue of the restaurant owner and head waiter.

Leaving the restaurant shortly before 5.00pm it had been a long, drawn-out meal, very expensive, but likely to be worthwhile with all three of the potential clients showing positive signs of moving their extensive accounts to Miles, Mackenzie Partners. After handshakes all round Tom Ford set off for his temporary lodgings above an internet café on the corner of Willow Street and Paul Street in the up-and-coming Shoreditch area.

It was only a short distance by foot from Old Street station and should only take a few minutes by tube then a short walk but for Tom Ford nothing was straightforward. Least of all when using public transport. He liked to know where he was at all times and that nobody was ever following. He had suffered in the past from poor anti surveillance but now was not the time. And sure enough, there was someone he had seen more than once since leaving the restaurant. It may be nothing but the doubter inside himself needed to know.

As Tom left the company of Mr Perkins, he walked along the busy street quickly losing himself amongst the throng of Londoners making their way home in the light rain. His first stop was the Estate Agents at the end of the road where Tom spent several minutes weighing up the benefits of renting in Camden Town as opposed to paying the lavish prices of a newly developed apartment on the Isle of Dogs. Turning swiftly and at some pace Tom made his way towards Old Street underground station but not before a split-second survey of the surrounding area. Crowds, movement, like cattle but it is the man stood still on the opposite side that stands out. Jeans, dark hooded top, dark blue, maybe black, mobile phone held to his ear but no lip movement. There was no talking into the phone. A one-way conversation maybe? Unlikely was his judgement.

Tom walked, stopped again at a queue waiting for the number 253 bus. The double decker bus arrived, and Tom waited for everyone to board then used the same bus to shield his movement. A sign up ahead indicated the underground station was near with no sign of the hooded man. Good, thought Tom as he arrived at the tube station and took up a position at the top of the escalator. Quickly opening his briefcase Tom removed a lightweight rainproof cagoul and placed it over his suit, at the same time folding his overcoat up and forcing it into the briefcase. He was now a different target than the one he was moments before. He accepted the briefcase was still there, but he now wore a lightweight green rainproof coat with hood pulled up as opposed to the dark blue overcoat from moments before. Waiting patiently in between the North and South tunnel entrances Tom's ploy worked and may well have saved his life. The hooded man was on the escalator heading towards him. Tom waited with his back to the escalator amongst a throng of passengers appearing to move with the crowd but in effect he was waiting for the confirmation he needed. And then it arrived. The hooded man, blue jeans, dark blue sports top with hood pulled up, walked past Tom, mobile phone in one hand, the other tucked away in a side pocket. Head movement suggested he was searching the crowd. He moved away towards the southbound platform and Tom followed at a discreet distance.

The platform was very congested. The City of London at this time of day is always congested. But give it a couple of hours and the whole City becomes like a ghost town. Unlike New York, a city that never sleeps, London does in fact enjoy a quiet evening and a decent sleep at night. But not at the moment.

The overhead display indicated two minutes before the arrival of the next southbound service. Tom watched as the hooded figure made his way through the crowd paying particular attention to anyone carrying any type of briefcase or bag. One minute was now showing on the display as Tom also pushed his way towards the front and in pursuit of the hooded male. Up ahead several young males were laughing and drinking from bottles. The hooded figure was just a few feet away and Tom was struggling through the packed platform in an attempt to catch up. A gust of hot air from the tunnel announced the train was imminent. Only two people now between Tom and the hooded male stood at the side of a businessman dressed not unlike Tom had been earlier.

A glint of metal and Tom saw the man was now holding a blade in place of the mobile phone. Tom pressed forward, through the drunken males who started to pull and push those around them. Another flash of light and more shouts from the drunks. But Tom was not bothered about the yobs. He saw two men in front. Holding each other. The hooded man was propping up the businessman, but the blade was missing from his hand. It was buried in the chest of his target. Maybe he was the target, maybe not thought Tom. It was a chance he was not prepared to take. A whoosh of more hot air was propelled onto the platform by the approaching train as Tom himself arrived at the side of the hooded figure and with one dip of the shoulder gave a solid nudge into the hip of the hooded man. Turning into the crowd and heading back towards the escalators Tom heard a train horn sound, people screaming, then emergency alarms ringing out. The incident caused severe delays to all trains on the Northern line that evening and would be the talk of the office the following morning. Tom had no intention of getting the tube for the foreseeable future.

Outside Old Street tube station Tom hailed a passing cab and within fifteen minutes he too was sat drinking a glass of red wine in his less than comfortable bedsit.

Chapter 6

Over the next three weeks Tom arrived at the office early and tended to leave late. He kept his head down. He chased up all his predecessor's clients, managed to bring in two new female clients, and spent a lot of time with his invaluable assistant Grace, who he had decided to call Gracie.

During that same period Grace too had thrown herself into work, and, on occasion, at the man she was working with. But so far, all her attempts at getting noticed for more than her office skills had not worked.

It was the last Friday of the month and Grace was sat at the Champagne bar at London St Pancras station. One perk she particularly enjoyed was the early finish all staff enjoyed each and every Friday. At 3pm exactly it was tools down for everyone. Everyone that wanted to relinquish their tools that was. Recently she had been staying fairly late most evenings responding to requests from Tom that she was not obliged to fulfil but nonetheless was happy to in the hope he would fulfil one of hers. Today, she had seen very little of him and had decided not to stay any later than 3.01 pm.

The booth at the Champagne bar overlooked the main thoroughfare within the station and Grace sipped her first glass of bubbly waiting for her date to arrive. If Tom wasn't going to ask her out, then she was going to make do with someone else.

Looking out over the St Pancras station shopping mall she saw just the person looking up in her direction. A smile and a raise of the glass brought a wave back in return and moments later Grace was joined in her booth by her date for the evening.

'Grace, hi. It's been too long darling', said Charley, as they both embraced.

'Yes, sorry. Been a bit over run at work. New boss, real dish, but slave driver. Cheers anyway'.

They clinked glasses and sat down opposite each other. Charley had briefly worked at Miles Mackenzie as a temp for a few weeks last year and both women had hit it off from the start. Neither woman seemed to talk much about their past, preferring to look to their futures, and had kept in regular contact when Charley left to take up a permanent role with a competitor.

'You look a little flushed', said Charley as Grace finished her first glass of champagne and ordered a second.

'I suppose I am. First early finish in weeks due to my new boss'.

'Yes, you naughty girl. We haven't caught up in ages. What's he got that I haven't?'.

'He's a man for a start', laughed Grace. She was beginning to relax and for the next hour both women went through their personal lives, advising each other on the options available, and what to do should either of them get lucky tonight. Grace had sat down at the bar at 3.30 pm and finally left the small booth arm in arm with her newest best friend Charley at 7.00pm. Both women were still roaring with laughter as they stumbled through the station towards the taxi rank and any onlooker if asked to describe their behaviour would describe them as being 'pissed'.

Charley took a cab from the rank outside St Pancras station, but Grace was adamant that she was fine on the tube. Both women lived on opposite sides of the river and sharing a taxi was neither practical nor cost effective. As Grace waved Charley off and watched the taxi disappear into the London evening, she suddenly found herself alone. It was late January and still quite dark at this time of the year. Grace wondered where everyone wanting taxis were and for a brief moment felt very vulnerable. A taxi pulled up alongside and the driver wound the window down and asked, 'Where to love?'.

Grace shook her head and replied, 'It's fine. I'm on the tube'.

It was a mistake.

As Grace headed towards the underground to make her way home two sets of eyes were watching her every move.

Chapter 7

London and its environs have a population of over nine million people and a good number of those are criminals.

Archie Bradshaw has lived in London all his life. Born and bred within the sound of Bow Bells, he considers himself to be a real cockney. There are some distant Scots connections, but he is a Londoner through and through. Having been brought up on the Isle of Dogs until leaving school he has, since that time, lived in most of its boroughs at some stage and spent time in the majority of the Met's Police stations. Now, at twenty-five, he was jobless, homeless, and penniless. And with a drugs habit of up to fifty quid a day to feed, he was in need of an easy victim before the withdrawals kicked in once again.

Bradshaw had been lurking in the shadows overlooking the taxi rank at the railway station, his preferred hunting ground, for the last two hours. Friday was always a rich pickings day. End of the working week. Londoners out for a drink or two, under the influence, all too willing to be helped up after a fall, very appreciative. It was his favourite day of the week. So far, he had managed to relieve a drunken businessman of his watch, a nice Armani timepiece at that. He would get a few quid for that no doubt. And, after another bad deed he had acquired a whole suitcase belonging to an elderly couple he had assisted into a taxi after the old girl had fallen off the footpath. The taxi driver was all too keen to get them into the back of the cab and on his way to Hendon that he neglected to check the young lad had put the case into the open boot. Archie had just closed the boot of the cab and given it two short taps indicating it was good to go. By the time they arrived at their address in Hendon most of their valuables were gone. The dirty underwear and mixed clothing would end up at the lost property office at the station no doubt but the two passports, a few items of ladies' jewellery, and a number of military medals that had once adorned the uniform of the proud old man would be circulating amongst the London criminal underworld.

The sixty euros and eighty dollars in foreign currency were safely tucked away in his jeans pocket and would be exchanged very shortly. But for now, he had another target. Two very drunk women had just arrived at the rank, and it looks like one is about to be left all on her lonesome.

Archie watched and waited.

There were no other people around apart from these two women. Then, as one drove off in a cab the other refused the next cab and set off on foot. Archie sensed another victim and decided to follow. There was potential in that designer handbag loosely slung over her shoulder. Checking his back pocket, the item was still there. It wasn't just for protection, it was also a helpful tool at times, the blade sharp enough to cut through the strap of any handbag in one quick swipe.

The Northern line tube is one of the oldest and deepest underground lines in London and there are two escalators to navigate before you arrive at the Northbound platform.

Grace headed down the first escalator with plenty of other passengers but walking along the tunnel towards the second she suddenly felt rather alone. Tipsy was her normal limit for alcohol consumption when travelling home alone. Tonight, she had gone too far and was quite drunk and somewhat queasy in the heavy underground atmosphere. Steadying herself, she leaned on the tunnel wall and took a few deep breaths, sucking in the dirty London air. Footsteps in the distance suddenly stopped. Looking up Grace saw there was nobody around but felt even more uneasy and started to walk at speed towards the second escalator. Letting the metal stairs take her deeper into the depths of Kings Cross she was nearly at the bottom when she became aware of someone else on the escalator heading towards her. A hooded figure. Grace walked off the end of the escalator and made her way towards the Northbound platform. Within seconds she heard quickened footsteps and continued onto the platform without looking back. She was shocked to find the platform empty.

'Shit', she whispered to herself and carried on walking, quickening her pace towards the far end.

She was sweating and felt physically sick. She could hear the footsteps getting louder, closer. Almost at the far end of the platform she felt a sharp tug at her shoulder.

Turning, Grace screamed at the sight before her. A young man had hold of her handbag.

'Give us the bag bitch!', cried the hooded man.

Grace couldn't move. She was mesmerised by the sight of what the man had in his right hand. A knife. All she could focus on was the knife. Memories of a distant past returned. Other men, a knife, a dark place. Grace thought she was over that bad experience. Clearly, she wasn't. She would have willingly given up the bag if she could have but her brain was so fuddled it was not sending out the correct messages to the rest of her body.

'The fucking bag bitch. Now!'.

Grace sank to her knees and started to sob as the hooded figure raised the knife. But without any warning this man's head impacted with the wall. There was blood splattered on the wall as his eye seemed to explode in a sea of red. His grip on her bag loosened and he spun around to slash out at another passenger. A man in a suit was now the focus of her attacker's attention. But this man wasn't backing away. The hooded figure took another swipe with his knife, but his arm was seized by the businessman who, in one swift movement, twisted his wrist with one hand before using his other to strike a blow to the attacker's elbow.

The resulting 'snap', the sound of bone breaking was all too much for Grace who proceed to vomit onto the platform. The hooded figure was screaming now, his right arm bent at an unnatural angle. With another sudden movement the head of the hooded figure impacted once more against the wall and then everything went silent. Grace threw up once more.

Then a familiar voice was heard, reassuring her. It was Tom.

'It's okay Grace. It's me, Tom. You are okay now. Police are on their way'.

Grace looked up and saw Tom's face looking down at her. She threw herself at him sobbing uncontrollably.

'Oh Tom. Thank goodness. I'm so scared'.

'Come on. Let's get out of here. I'm taking you home'.

Tom led Grace from the platform up the escalators and towards the underground exit. The further up they got the more people there were and just as they arrived at the top of the second escalator with a number of other passengers alighting from other lines a number of Police officers were running into the station and heading down towards the deep Northern line.

Tom escorted Grace back to the taxi rank where a number of cabs were waiting. He helped Grace into the back of the cab and sat beside her.

'Where to guv?', asked the cabbie.

Tom looked at Grace who managed to control herself and gave the driver an address in Highgate.

Twenty minutes later the cab pulled up outside Grace's apartment and Tom helped her out.

'Don't go, please', asked Grace.

Tom nodded, 'Sure', and paid the driver.

'Where are your keys Grace?'.

Fumbling around her handbag for what seemed like an age Grace eventually found what she was looking for and handed Tom the largest bunch of keys he'd ever seen.

'All these?', he asked with a cheeky grin. 'Who are you Grace Canning?'.

This brought a little smile to her face as she replied, 'Sorry. There are so many locks'.

And sure enough, there were so many locks to open. Each key had a number painted on it to help. There were two keys required for the outer door, another key for the internal passage door. One for the letterbox, two for the back door, and two for her apartment door. A total of eight keys, although only five were actually required before access was gained to the apartment.

After the apartment door was finally opened Tom found the light switch, closed the door, and had a quick look around. As he emerged from the bathroom he announced, 'All clear'.

Grace suddenly ran to him and wrapped her arms around his neck continuing her uncontrollable sobbing. Tom held her tight until her shoulders stopped jumping up and down and he was sure she had regained something of her composure. Breaking from him Grace took a couple of steps back, folded her arms, and said in a broken voice.

'Thanks again Tom. You saved my life..... I think'.

'Don't be silly. It was just a youth after your bag'.

'He had a knife. Should I call the Police Tom?'.

'Let me make you a cup of coffee. I'll sort everything out with the Police tomorrow. Leave it with me'.

'But....', Grace started to protest but Tom led her towards her sofa, sat her down, and placed a throw on her legs.

'Just sit and take it easy Grace. You're still in shock. I'll get us both a coffee'.

Grace wiped her eyes and nodded.

Tom headed to the small kitchen area and put the kettle on. A few minutes later Tom returned to the sofa carrying two cups of steaming coffee. Looking down at the woman in front of him he smiled. Grace was fast asleep. Exhausted no doubt by the whole experience. Had he misjudged her? He thought she was a stronger person than the woman he had rescued.

Putting the two cups gently down on a side table Tom picked up a throw from one end of the sofa and gently laid it over the sleeping Grace.

As Grace slept Tom sipped his coffee. He was deep in thought.

Coffee finished he made himself comfortable on the floor beside her and closed his eyes.

Chapter 8

When Archie Bradshaw came out of his unconscious state, he was no longer on the Kings Cross Northern Line. He was handcuffed to a bed at St Thomas' hospital. His unbroken arm was cuffed to the bed rail whilst his broken arm was in plaster which ran from his wrist all the way up to his armpit. A uniformed Police officer was stood at the door, and he appeared to be alone in a side room. Opening his eyes caused his head to hurt. He was aware of bandage on his head. Then the pain kicked in at his elbow. Fuck, it hurt. He remembered the lady with the bag. The bitch wouldn't let go. Then everything went black. No, there was a man first. Then everything went black.

'Well. Look who we have here. Archie Bradshaw, all beaten up by a lady with a handbag'.

Another person was in the room and had been sat at the far end. Bradshaw recognised the man, a Cop he had had dealings with before.

'Fuck off Carter, you wanker. I was beat up by a fucking maniac. I'm the victim. You should be looking for a crazy man'.

Detective Constable Dave Carter was a ten-year serving officer on the BTP's Robbery team. The British Transport Police had jurisdiction over any crime committed on London's rail network and were responsible for Policing the whole of the National railway system as well as the London Underground.

DC Carter sat on the edge of the bed facing Bradshaw. He had an intense look on his face. Carter was a thief taker, good at his job, and could read people. He had been a detective for six years. He loved his job and was one of those individuals who was confident in his own abilities. Each day at work whatever the challenge he knew he would face it and overcome it. At 5.11, he was not the tallest in the pack but having been on the verge of turning pro as a boxer in his youth before injury to his left hand forced a change of career, he could mix it with the best of them. At thirty-four years old Carter was ready for a new challenge. Promotion to Uniform Sergeant was in the pipeline, a possibility of a move out of London, somewhere more rural. He had turned it down twice, but his Area Commander had seen potential in him. Wanted him to branch out, experience the BTP outside of London before bringing it back into the Capital and hopefully further promotion. But first, he needed to clear up this spate of outstanding robberies. And he was looking at his prime suspect.

'Thing is Archie, I'd prefer you called me DC Carter, or Mr Carter', replied the detective, his manner serious but calm.

'Piss off. You're not a real cop anyway'.

'Is that right Archie'.

Carter moved further up the bed until he was sat on the unbroken arm of Archie Bradshaw. With a pair of rigid handcuffs connecting his wrist to the bedframe the weight of the solid detective caused the cuffs to put pressure onto Bradshaw's wrist and the subsequent pain was excruciating. Sitting on his arm Carter quickly covered the mouth of the prisoner preventing his scream from escaping. As Archie's eyes grew wide with terror Carter whispered into his ear.

'Show me some respect and I'll treat you like the human being you most certainly are not. Understand?'.

Bradshaw nodded vigorously.

Carter removed his hand and stood from the bed. Taking out a small bottle of anti-bacterial liquid he applied a small amount and rubbed his hands together. With his hands now dry Carter removed a plastic bag from his pocket. The bag was a Police exhibit bag and inside was a black handled lock knife.

'I suppose I should remind you that you are still under caution, so I'll go through it again if you wish'. Carter went through the Police caution in full just to be sure.

'Recognise this Archie?'.

Carter held up the exhibit bag containing the lock knife.

'Er..Nope'.

The detective raised his eyebrow and sighed.

'Okay, okay. It's mine. It's for protection but I don't use it', sighed the patient.

'Then how do you explain this?'.

Carter removed some photos from his inside pocket and started to lay them out on the bed on front of Bradshaw.

The first photograph showed a picture of a male approaching the Kings Cross tube entrance. It was clearly showing Bradshaw's face and distinctive clothing.

'Who is this?'.

'Could be me', replied Bradshaw.

'And this'.

Carter placed a second photo down showing Bradshaw once more. This time on an empty Northern line platform.

'Ok. So it's me. I'm on my own. So what'.

'Then tell me what you are doing here please'.

This time Carter placed a photo down in front of Bradshaw that clearly shows him approaching a lone woman on the same platform. Bradshaw is holding a knife in one hand whilst tugging at the strap of a woman's handbag. The woman appears to be on her knees.

'No comment. I want my brief now'.

'Of course, Archie. Thing is we are going to talk a lot more about this when you are released back to the nick. But for now, we are struggling to find this woman and are concerned for her safety and wellbeing. Can you tell us anything else that might help us find her Archie? It may well help you in the long term'.

'Bollocks', replied Archie, grinning. 'Without her you've got nothing Carter. Sorry, DC Carter'.

'You are so right Archie. Well, almost anyway. We do have the knife, an offensive weapon found on your person'. Carter paused at the door momentarily before continuing as if he had just remembered something important.

'Oh, and the Armani watch, some dollars, Euros, a lot of ladies' jewellery and some war medals. Thing is Archie, there is CCTV everywhere these days. Mr and Mrs Chambers have been very helpful, as has Mr Cotton. They are fairly local, and I've got statements from all three about their stolen gear already. Catch you later'.

As Carter left laughing to himself loud enough so that Bradshaw could hear a suited man waited outside next to the Uniform Cop. This was no Police Officer, but Carter's bosses had made it perfectly clear that he was to cooperate with him and give him whatever assistance he required.

'Well. Any joy from the injured party'.

The suited man spoke like he was from a well to do area. Definitely public school educated. You could tell just by looking at him. He was a government man, well connected no doubt. Some sort of spook. Tread carefully, Carter told himself.

'A little sir. He's bang to rights for a number of Robberies on the Underground which I'm sure I'll get sufficient evidence to prove, but I didn't push him on the stranger who beat him up'.

'Good. Do you have the photograph for me?'.

Carter reached back into his overcoat pocket and pulled out two photographs of the Robbery scene on the Northern line platform. The first showed Bradshaw lying unconscious on the platform whilst the woman was being helped up by a man dressed like a businessman. The second showed the same couple walking away from the prone Bradshaw and gave a visual of the pair from their shoulders up. The pictures were a little grainy. He handed them over to the Government man.

'Can I ask what this is about Sir, and will you give me the identity of the couple in the photo if you find them?'.

'No', replied the government man as he turned the door handle and walked in to see the broken Archie Bradshaw.

Chapter 9

Grace Canning woke early. She was confused and uncomfortable at first, feeling as if she was being crushed by a big weight. It was still dark outside and not yet light, so it took a minute or so for her to adjust to her surroundings. She was on the sofa. It was quite a large comfortable sofa made from high end fabric and would normally offer her plenty of space. But today there was someone else on the sofa with her. Tom, her boss, was behind her as they lay spoon like on her sofa with just a blanket covering them both.

Memories of the night before started to flood in. The drinks with Charley. That was good. Then the man with a knife. That was bad. Then Tom arrived and saved her. That was good. He beat up the man with the knife. Was that good? She wasn't sure.

She remembers Tom brought her home. Made her coffee. She needed something stronger and had Brandy in her coffee. They both did. Then they had brandy in glasses. Grace wouldn't let Tom leave. She was too scared she had told him and virtually begged him to stay. And now here he was. They were entwined together.

Had they kissed? She wasn't sure. Grace hoped they had. They must have. Her skirt. Where was her skirt. She was still wearing her blouse which was loosened. She still wore a bra, had her knickers on, unfortunately she thought to herself. All of yesterday's woes seemed worth it at this very moment in time. She was in the arms of the man she desired. A man who had come to her rescue. He was still breathing deeply with a regular tone and was in a deep sleep. Grace moved her right hand gently down to her side and felt Tom's trousers. He was still clothed. That was unfortunate too. Still, it was a start.

Then Grace had something of a wicked idea. Slowly and very gently she unbuttoned her blouse, pausing after each button until her garment was completely open. Then, waiting until she was sure Tom was still in a deep sleep, she carefully manoeuvred his arm until she was able to guide his hand to rest on her left breast. It felt wonderful. Grace closed her eyes and drifted off back into a contented sleep. But a slight movement brought her back. Tom had moved but his hand had remained in place. In fact, it was no longer resting there. Tom now had a hold of her breast. Grace became aroused, her nipple hardened, and she was in something of state. Her breathing became heavy. Another movement, a caress, a massaging of her bosom caused her to gasp, 'Oh god'. Grace felt a kiss on the back of her neck and knew then that Tom wanted her as much as she wanted him. Turning onto her back their lips met in a passionate kiss that lingered for what seemed like an age. Tom knew exactly what he was doing and moved slowly down from her neck kissing his way as he went. How did he know she liked that? By the time he had reached his destination Grace was panting so heavily it was hard to catch her breath. She could feel her panties slowly being removed. Grace opened herself up to Tom. She was so ready for him.

'Oh Tom', she cried.

'Grace', called Tom, shaking her. 'Grace, wake up. I have to go'.

Opening her eyes, Grace was momentarily confused. Tom was stood, fully clothed, looking down on her. Shouldn't he be on top of her.

'Oh god. It was a dream', she said out loud.

'I'm afraid it wasn't', replied Tom, holding a cup of hot steaming coffee. 'Here, take this'.

'It wasn't', questioned Grace, peering down under the blanket that covered her. The blouse was actually completely open and her skirt nowhere to be seen.

'I'm afraid not Grace. You had something of an ordeal on the underground yesterday. I happened to be about and managed to fend off the attacker. I slept in the chair over there. Hope you don't mind'.

A little flushed now, Grace sat up spilling a little of her coffee.

'On the chair?', she asked.

'Yes. I took a couple of blankets from the bedroom after you fell asleep on the sofa and made us both comfortable'.

'Thank you, Tom', replied Grace, more than a little disappointed. But then her hopes were raised once more as her hunk of a boss knelt down before her, took her face in his hands, and kissed her gently.

'Take it easy today, Grace. Call me if you need anything. Anything at all'.

It was a gentle kiss on her forehead, but still a kiss, nonetheless.

'Ok, I will', she whispered back.

As Tom closed the door behind him Grace put her coffee down and made herself comfortable on the sofa once more. Thoughts of Tom filled her head again. Erotic thoughts of passion consumed her. Grace closed her eyes, reached down and placed her hand inside her wet pants. She needed release and decided to finish what Tom had started a few minutes earlier, albeit in a dream.

'Oh god Tom', she cried out bringing herself to a speedy climax. 'Who are you?'.

Chapter 10

An hour after leaving Grace and following his usual circuitous route, Tom arrived at Paddington Railway station where he took a cab from the rank. Forty-five minutes after leaving the station he alighted the cab at Richmond Park. It was a chilly morning with the usual number of runners, dog walkers, and parents pushing their children. There was a smell of freshly cut grass in the air which he thought unusual given the time of year. Purchasing a takeaway latte from what was becoming his regular coffee van at the entrance he took up a position on a bench with a good view of the park gates and surrounding area.

An hour later Tom entered an address on Portland Terrace on the edge of Richmond Green. Using an electronic key fob, the front gates rolled back allowing him entry onto the front driveway. As the gates closed behind him, he thoroughly checked the two vehicles that were parked up. The silver-coloured Audi 4x4 stood alongside the smaller but faster black BMW Z3. Checking the underside of both motor cars, their locking mechanisms, exhaust systems, and tyre positions, all seemed to be as he had last left them one week ago. Apart from the odd damp patch on the rear patio from a likely downpour all was as it should be. The covert CCTV system would shortly confirm that the only visitors to this particular address during the last seven days apart from himself was the local postman, whom he had made a point of watching on several occasions, and a local as yet unidentified cat.

Number three Portland Terrace, Richmond, is an impressive building whichever way you look at it. With eight bedrooms, four separate reception rooms, a gymnasium, sauna, and basement pool it was the property of someone with serious wealth. Once owned by a knight of the realm it was last valued three years ago at 7.5 million pounds. Its white façade shone like a beacon over 'The Green' and often caused passers-by to stare up at the impressive building, one of only three

Georgian show homes among numerous other later, council-built properties.

How Tom came to have the key to such a place eluded him at the moment. His memories were sketchy and whilst he was aware of spending some recent time at the place, there were not many long-term memories. For now, he had possession of this beautiful fortress. And a fortress it was.

There were photographs everywhere. Family photographs depicting weddings, holidays, graduations. Fun times everywhere on display. Children alongside adults young and old. A girl and two boys were prominent in many of the scenes on display but no matter how closely he looked at the pictures, they invoked no personal memories.

Tom took the stairs two at a time and at the top of the first floor he stood at the first door on his left. The internal décor was clean and rather neutral. The high ceilings were all a matt white as were all the walls on the ground floor giving it something of a medical feel. The second floor had a similar theme but unlike the ground floor this level had all its walls painted in a very light duck egg blue. The top floor housing most of the bedrooms had a dull rose colour everywhere. Tom often wondered about the strange colourings and whether this had been down to him or a previous occupier. Were the colours supposed to represent something, a country's flag maybe. He didn't know. Tom actually liked the minimalist approach to the furnishings, with no wallpaper anywhere, and very little in the way of unnecessary fixtures and fittings. The colour coded levels were also a help in remembering where everything was.

Punching in a five-digit code Tom turned the handle and entered through the door to one of the rear facing bedrooms. In actual fact the room had not been a bedroom for many years. It was in effect his control room and CCTV hub. Banks of monitors were displaying images of all the internal rooms and a number of external positions. The whole place inside and out was covered. Two laptops were closed but linked together and to a large central processor. Lifting the lid on the first laptop it came to life instantly. The screen was split into sixteen windows each displaying a different image of the property. Tom removed a small red coloured memory stick from the laptop. Taking his keys from his pocket he unhooked an identical blue coloured memory stick and inserted this into the laptop before hooking the previous stick back onto his key ring. The memory stick housed the last seven days' worth of CCTV recordings and would allow Tom to quickly check whether anything untoward had occurred.

First though, he needed a shower and a change of clothes. He left his control room, headed up to the top floor, and straight into a hot steaming 360-degree surround shower cubicle. As the hot steamy liquid cascaded down over Tom's body he began to remember. Visions of other showers taken appeared inside his head. Images of bodies lying prone, lifeless, in faraway cities. Blood on his hands. A need to cleanse.

'Who am I?', he said in a low tone.

A sudden thought caused Tom to straighten.

Switching off the shower he grabbed a towel and ran to the control room. Something was not right. Something out of place. Inserting the small red memory stick into the second laptop he waited until the program had completed and confirmed his instinct. There had been a breach. Sector 8 had been breached at 02.13 am three days ago. Sector 8 covered the rear of the property near the garden gate in the far, right hand corner. Scrolling through the recording Tom found what he was looking for within a few minutes. A shadowy figure could be seen climbing over the wall at 02.13. The figure, all in black, and pretty unidentifiable from a facial point of view, did not approach the property. Tom watched as the figure stood in the far corner, dipping in and out of the shadows, for just over twenty minutes. There was no attempt to enter the house. Not even any attempt to move closer.

'What are you up to?', Tom spoke to himself.

At 02.39 the dark figure climbed back over the wall. It was an eight-foot wall and Tom wondered how the intruder had managed it so effortlessly. Chain ladder, knotted rope maybe. If so, this was a professional who would no doubt be back. The red light on the screen caused Tom to pause the visual. As the figure reached the top of the wall they turned and were clearly holding something. Something that had an infra-red signal. Tom rewound the footage and this time instead of focussing on the intruder he focussed his attention all over the screen.

And there it was. There was a second red dot in the picture. A moving red dot. Tom's first thought was that a weapon was searching for its target but on closer inspection he found that the dot was attached to an object.

An object that was hovering at the top of his property.

A drone. It had to be.

A damp patch at the rear. That's what was out of place.

Quickly dressing, Tom put on his running gear, a lightweight hooded zip top, and an old pair of grey Nike running shoes. From his bedside drawer he removed a small Sig P365 handgun, checked the magazine, cocked it and attached an even smaller suppressor to its muzzle. Placing the pistol into the side pocket of his hooded top Tom left the house via the back door and went out into the rear garden.

Checking the far end there was no damage to the gate or garden wall and only the most highly trained eye would have noticed the indentations left in the well-manicured lawn.

Perhaps the intruder was not as professional as he first thought but nonetheless, they were an intruder. An unwanted guest. Looking back towards the rear of the property Tom instantly saw what was out of place. A wet patch on the ground below the rear ground floor window. It shouldn't be there. The drainage pipe next to the patch takes all the rainwater away. Looking up, Tom saw that the pipe was slightly askew at the top. Something had nudged the guttering along the roof edge and there must be a slight gap causing at least some of the water to cascade down.

The drone.

Tom started to run. He needed exercise. He also needed to think.

As Tom jogged around Richmond Park there was only one thing on his mind. The Intruder.

'Who are you?', he kept asking himself.

Chapter 11

Archie Bradshaw stood before the Custody Sergeant who looked over at DC Carter and nodded.

'Archie. Listen to what the Sergeant has to say. It's important you listen'.

Bradshaw said nothing responding with a shrug of the shoulders.

'Archibald Bradshaw. You are charged with the following offences. You do not have to say anything. But it may harm your defence if you fail to mention now anything you later rely on in court. Anything you do say may be used in evidence'.

After a brief pause the young female Custody Sergeant continued with her spiel and read out three charges, all relating to the night of his arrest the previous week. There were two theft charges relating to the Armani watch and a suitcase containing cash and jewellery plus a further charge of possessing an offensive weapon. The victim in relation to the knifepoint robbery had yet to come forward and was still being investigated by the Detective.

'Sign here', instructed the Sergeant.

Carter pointed to the screen in front and made sure Bradshaw knew exactly where he was to put his mark. There was no paperwork to sign just a screen. All records were held electronically in the majority of most English custody suites. Everything was going digital.

'You are on bail to appear at Westminster Magistrates Court at 10 am on the 21st of February in relation to these charges. Further to this, you are also being bailed pending further enquiries into an offence of Robbery to return here at St Pancras Police station on the 14th February at 6 pm. Understand?'.

'No comment', replied a subdued Archie Bradshaw.

His arm was still in plaster, he was taking numerous painkillers, and Bradshaw was still something of a broken man. However, his mood improved slightly when he realised he was not going straight into the remand system, as both he and DC Carter had expected.

'Sarge. I raised a number of concerns about bail', said the surprised Detective.

'He has an address, does he not?'.

'He does', nodded Carter.

'He's not on bail for anything else and hasn't committed any offences whilst on bail. Not within the last year anyway', she went on.

'True, but I am investigating a serious robbery sarge, and a number of other thefts on the underground which I believe he is responsible for'.

'Not enough for me Detective. He's skating on thin ice but at the moment he's not done enough for me to send him down at the taxpayer's expense. Maybe the Westminster magistrates will have a different view. Please show him out'.

An unhappy Dave Carter escorted an uplifted Archie Bradshaw from the custody area. As he watched Bradshaw walk away, he watched him closely. Bradshaw turned towards the detective and with a wide smile gave the detective a little wave then grabbed his crotch area to throw one last insult.

Carter laughed and gave him the finger. His time would come. He was sure of it. Carter watched his prime robbery suspect disappear into the London populace once more.

Bradshaw had a smile on his face as he made his way through the crowds around St Pancras and headed towards Camden Town and the hovel that he called home. Unfortunately for Bradshaw, as Carter's eyes stopped tracking him, other sets of eyes were upon him. More intense, sinister eyes. His uplifted mood was about to turn South.

Chapter 12

Tom followed at a safe distance. He was a professional and felt sure there was no chance of being spotted by an amateur thief, but he was not the only one watching Bradshaw. Another pair of eyes were following the young rogue through the streets of London.

194 Maiden Lane, London, is an old, terraced property on the edge of Kings Cross and Camden. It was a property that had seen better days and was now a multi occupational residence housing some of the capital's most downtrodden individuals. Archie's room was situated on the ground floor, one of four bedsits all owned by an anonymous landlord who rarely visited other than to evict nonpayers. This was a rare event however, as all were on varying levels of government benefits and the rent in most cases was completely taken care of by the local authority.

Archie was in buoyant mood as he tossed his charge sheet onto the floor and attempted to close his bedsit door behind him. Something was preventing the door close. Nothing worked properly in this hole. He pushed a little harder, but it still wouldn't budge. Opening the door wide he jumped back, startled to see a woman stood in the doorway, her foot the obvious blockage.

It took Archie a few seconds but eventually he regained his composure.

'What the fuck do you want?'.

The woman, older than himself but not much older he considered. She would be no match for Archie. There was no threat here. There may even be an opportunity coming his way. Dressed all in leather she was carrying a full-face motorcycle helmet. Archie watched as she kicked the door closed behind her.

She was a looker too. Had he seen her before somewhere? Perhaps he owed her some money. Reaching for his back pocket his lock knife was no longer available. Still, she would pose no threat, he was sure.

'Do you know who I am?', asked the leather clad biker, a certain tone in her voice that Archie didn't like.

'You're making a big mis…..'.

The impact of helmet on jaw sent a shocked Archie stumbling backwards. He managed to grab the edge of the chair at the window, breaking his fall.

'You fucking bitch. I'm gonna kill you', he screamed. Archie lunged at her but was met by a second swipe of hard plastic. This time his nose exploded in a sea of red. Before he could regain any sort of composure, he found his good arm in a hold that was causing him so much pain he pleaded with the biker for release.

'Please, not the other arm, please', he begged.

'One more time. Do you know who I am?', screamed the biker.

'No. I…I don't think so'.

There was a gentle squeeze of Archies wrist which was looking like the head of a swan causing shooting pain to surge through his body.

'No, no. For fuck sake. I have no fucking idea who you are or what you want'.

When release came Archie backed away from this biker chick. She was a maniac. As he rubbed his wrist in an attempt to get the blood circulating once more, she leaned in and whispered in his ear. Archie flinched as she spoke.

'Good. Keep it that way. I don't want to come back. If I do. You're a dead man'.

Archie looked up from his position on the floor as she calmly replaced her helmet before walking out his door.

Tom held his position keeping the address on Maiden Lane in view. Standing amongst a mixed group of local commuters waiting for a bus he was about to step out and make his way across the road when his attention was drawn to a car coming to a sudden stop in the road outside the address that Bradshaw had entered. A suited man alighted from the vehicle and strode purposefully towards the front door. As he was about to attempt to attract someone's attention inside the front door opened and a biker in full leathers brushed past him. The man paid little attention to the biker, grateful that entry had so easily been obtained.

Tom returned to the group and decided to wait. The man had a military bearing. An official look. Police perhaps. Tom would wait.

Archie had no sooner stemmed the flow of blood from his smashed nose when another individual appeared at his door.

'Archibald Bradshaw', asked the suited man stood at his open door.

'Who wants to know?', replied Archie in a nasal drawl as he held his head up at an angle towards the ceiling.

The man wore a long overcoat over his suit and had a sinister air about him thought Archie. He watched as the man, a white man, about 45 years old, athletically built, took out a pair of brown leather gloves and slowly placed them on his hands watching Archie closely as he did so. When he had completed his task, he reached inside his coat and removed a grainy photograph. As his overcoat was moved to one side Archie saw that the man was armed. He had a holstered pistol on his belt. When the man spoke again it startled Archie.

'Look at this and tell me if you know the two other people in the photo'.

The image was of Archie on the underground platform. A man and a woman were also in the picture. He recognised the scene and remembered the attempted robbery on the tube.

'Well', asked the man. His tone was sharp, expectant.

'Er...no I don't know them. I just tried to rob the woman, but...'

'You're running out of time son'.

'The woman. She was here. Just now. A biker, all in leather. She did this to me'.

Archie removed the tissue from his blooded nose to show his second visitor, but he had gone and taken the picture with him.

Tom changed his position and found a passing cab which he persuaded to park up and wait for his colleague who was getting changed across the road. The cabbie was happy to wait as long as Tom was happy to pay.

'The clock is ticking mate'.

'No worries. She won't be long'.

The cab gave Tom a good view of Bradshaw's address and sure enough within two minutes of the official looking man entering, he came running out. Tom watched as he made a call on his mobile before being picked up by the same car that had dropped him off earlier.

Tom had seen enough.

'Ok driver. Let's go. She's not coming', Tom said to the cabbie.

'Where to mate?'.

'Highgate cemetery please'.

Chapter 13

Tom gave the cabbie a generous tip as he left the cab and headed into the cemetery. The cemetery itself has over 170, 000 residents and is visited by thousands of visitors every day. The most notable grave that attracts the majority of curious visitors is that of Karl Marx. For Tom, apart from using it as part of his circuitous routine, he often found himself drawn to the war graves memorial. A screen dedicated to those whose graves could not be marked by headstones are listed on the memorial erected near the Cross of Sacrifice in the west cemetery. Standing in silence, Tom felt a connection. Memories of long hikes over harsh mountainous terrain filled his head. Sleeping outdoors under canvass, living off the land, lying in wait, a rifle his only companion. Memories from a former life perhaps?

Approaching footsteps caused Tom to move on without looking back. The footsteps stopped, were not following, and clearly no threat. Speeding up his movement he set off towards his target address.

Tom walked straight up the steps and pressed the top button. He heard a buzzer sound in the distance and waited. Turning around Tom took in the view of the passing traffic. A motorcycle was parked on the roadside a few doors down amongst a row of motor cars. The cars were a mix of new and old, neutral colours. Some were high performance, but most were small engine, city commuter size vehicles. His eyes were drawn back towards the motorcycle. A 750 cc Honda. Very slick, all black. Fast.

A voice brought his attention back to the intercom.

'Hello', came an electronic sounding voice. Tom immediately recognised Gracie's voice.

'Hi Grace. It's me, Tom'.

'Hi….Tom. Come on up'. There was a pause in between the greeting and his name, Grace obviously not expecting a visit.

A buzzer allowed Tom to advance through the outer door before climbing up the steps to her top floor apartment.

Arriving at the door Tom was greeted by Grace stood in the open doorway inviting him in.

Grace seemed pleased to see Tom. She had missed him in work today.

'Hello stranger. I missed you in work today. What have you been up to Mr Ford?', enquired the smiling Grace. She had one eyebrow raised indicating she suspected he had been skipping work.

'I've been visiting clients Miss Canning. I promise'.

Grace closed the door and turned. Tom was staring at her. Looking her up and down. Grace, slightly amused, placed a hand on hip and gave a cheeky little pose.

'You want a picture Mr Ford?', she said.

There was no initial response from Tom. He was still staring at her. At her leather trousers.

'Are you a biker Gracie?', asked Tom.

Grace noticed his stare was not one of desire as she had first thought and stood there a little confused.

'I might be. Why?', her voice low and drawn out.

'Because....It really suits you. Wow!'.

Grace saw that Tom had a grin like a Cheshire cat on his face. Starting to blush she was relieved inside. She hadn't had time to change since returning from her recent trip, but Tom seemed to have a genuine like for the way she looked. Maybe he felt the same way she did. His next remark almost caused her to choke and started a coughing fit in her.

'I'd like to ride you Gracie....sorry, I mean I'd like to ride with you'.

Tom realised what he had said almost immediately but it was too late. Grace started to cough and choke in response to his offer. And deep down Tom would in fact love to both take a ride with and on the attractive woman before him, now struggling to breathe.

Patting her gently on her back, Grace bent over gasping for air. Tom stopped the patting but placed an arm around her shoulders and attempted to reassure her and regain some sort of composure. He knew he had actually said what he was thinking.

'Sorry Gracie, I didn't mean to shock you with my poor choice of words'.

Grace's breathing returned to normal.

Standing, she found herself face to face with Tom, his right arm still around her shoulders. Both Grace and Tom stood facing each other. Grace could feel his breath on her, smell his cologne. She recognised the fragrance but couldn't place its name. She felt another arm move around her waist, gently pulling her in closer. Grace didn't resist, she let Tom take control. She wanted him to make a move, was desperate for him to make a move. Her eyes were burning into his. Telepathically Grace was begging this man to take her. She wanted his lips on hers. And then, closing her eyes, Grace gently tipped her head to one side and leaned in hoping she had not interpreted this incorrectly.

She hadn't.

Tom's lips were warm and soft on hers. His gentle kiss was received with a tentative caress of the back of his neck. Grace's encouragement worked and their kiss became more passionate. Mouths opened up and Grace felt his tongue inside her own. Responding in kind she realised that Tom was very aroused. He was holding her in a tight embrace, his hand moving south until it rested on her left buttock. Grace gave out a very slight groan and pushed her face harder against his. Tom guided Grace towards the sofa and they continued their kissing in a little more comfort. Grace was happy to let Tom take the lead but felt he was being a little too cautious. She wanted his hands in other places. On her body. Breaking from his kiss she took his hand and placed it on her breast. She wore a thin cotton T-shirt and this gave Tom no doubt in what Grace wanted from him. To reinforce this Grace whispered in his ear.

'It's ok Tom. Do what you want'.

Grace returned her lips to his as Tom squeezed her breast. Grace gasped as Tom became more confident in his caresses.

A sudden buzzing noise from the door's intercom system caused them both to bolt upright. Straightening herself Grace turned to Tom and whispered, 'Stay there'.

Tom nodded with a smile on his face and gave her the thumbs up.

Grace went to the front door to her flat and picked up the phone. Disappointment flowed through her whole body as she rested her head on the door and knew her passionate moment with Tom had come to an end. It was her friend Charley.

'Grace, It's me, Charley. Can I come in?'.

'Is everything ok Charley because….'.

'He's left me Grace', blurted out the voice on the other end of the phone before the sound of sobbing kicked in.

'Come on up Charley'.

She turned towards Tom, and mouthed the words, 'Sorry' raising both arms in a gesture that also said, What else can I do?

Grace pressed the button allowing Charley entry and opened the front door. Within seconds a tearful Charley appeared flinging her arms around Grace.

'Come on through', said Grace leading Charley into her small lounge.

Tom was stood and had heard enough of the exchange to realise that it was time for him to leave, disappointment showing all over his face as the two women appeared.

'Oh, sorry. I didn't realise you had company Grace', sobbed Charley,

'I was just leaving anyway. It's getting late. I'll catch up with you in work tomorrow Miss Canning'.

Charley giggled amid her sobs and looked over at Grace who she saw was staring at her boss.

'Ok Mr Ford, see you tomorrow. Thanks for the......support'.

Charley giggled again and Tom went a little red in the face as he looked over and saw that she was staring at him a little too intently. Grace walked Tom out into the vestibule area outside her front door and whispered, 'Sorry about this'.

Tom smiled back and gave Grace a quick peck on her cheek. 'Me too', then disappeared down the stairs and out the front door.

As Grace returned to her friend, Charley was stood at her window looking out into the street. She was watching Tom who had walked over towards a motorcycle and seemed to be checking it over. Turning to her friend she asked, 'Have I interrupted something?'.

'Yes', replied Grace. 'Yes, you most certainly have'.

'Sorry', sobbed Charley.

'Never mind. Glass of wine?'.

'Please', said Charley.

Chapter 14

Dave Carter had been in the CID office for a good hour before most of his colleagues turned in.

There was only two days to go before that twat Archie Bradshaw answered Police bail and Carter was still struggling to get any evidence to prove the Attempted Robbery.

Carter knew Bradshaw had a connection to Scotland and was a frequent visitor, very surprising considering his position in the food chain. As a last-ditch attempt Carter had contacted his old mate Danny Fairbank at the Glasgow CID office to see if he could come up with something. The good thing about the BTP was that as a National Police Force getting information and making requests of officers in other parts of the UK was a lot easier. Carter was about to find out just how lucky he was as far as this quirky nature of the BTP went.

Snatching at the phone Carter felt sure this was his call and sure enough the thick Scottish accent on the other end of the line confirmed it.

'Danny, how the devil are you? Still chomping on haggis and watching Braveheart every Saturday?'.

'Aye. Can't beat an evening with Mel and a dram of the hard stuff', laughed the Scottish officer.

'Any joy with Archie Bradshaw?'.

'Well. Sort of Davie boy. Sort of'.

'I'm on a timescale here Danny. Anything will help'.

'Well, we have a lot of intel on an Archie Duncan Bradshaw but nothing on an Archie Bradshaw and the picture you sent doesn't match our own Archibald'.

'Bugger', cursed a despondent Dave Carter scratching his head and wondering if this was it.

'But', replied the Scot.

Carter's mood lifted slightly at the 'But' and sat upright waiting for his old mate to carry on.

'But when I was in our intel office this morning there was a DS from Police Scotland in with our intel guy. He works with Special Branch at the port and happened to see the picture. He was very excited Davie, and I mean very excited. Hard on excited if you know what I mean. He took the picture from me and said he may well be coming down to pay you a visit'.

'For fuck sake Danny. Tell me'.

'Ok. Well, he didn't know your Archie Bradshaw, but he did have a name for the guy in the picture. He says his name is Ross. Hugo Ross. At least that is what his passport said when he used it to cross into Scotland from Northern Ireland six months ago'.

'Got an address Danny?'.

'Sorry. And neither have the locals. But they are very interested in him'.

'Any idea why?'.

'Nope'.

'Ok. It's a start. Email me what you have when you get a break from the movie'.

'What movie?'.

'Braveheart, you big scotch haggis'.

Carter hung up laughing cutting off his old Glaswegian mate in mid expletive.

An hour later Carter was on his way to London's City Airport.

A call to the Border Force confirmed that a man using a passport in the name of Hugo Ross, D.O.B 16/12/85, entered England at London City Airport on the 10th of November the previous year. There was a Belfast address on the passport which Carter had looked up and it definitely exists. He would make a call to the PSNI, the Police Service of Northern Ireland later but for now he needed to check this man out for himself. If there was a trail to follow, he was going to find it. He had two days. The custody sergeant would need some extra evidence before authorising any charge or even an extension of Bradshaw's bail. But Carter had the bit between his teeth. As he pulled into the small parking area at the City Airport, he felt that he was onto something.

As Carter met a plain clothes Border Force Official at the passport control office his main suspect was boarding a train at Kings Cross Station heading for Glasgow. He was alone and looked like he had recently had a shower and combed his hair.

It was what was expected of him by his employer. He was to blend in. In his possession he had a black canvas holdall filled with clothing he had stolen from a charity clothing bank. He placed the bag in the luggage rack at the end of the carriage amongst many other cases and travel bags as he set off on his journey.

Archie Bradshaw sat in standard class towards the rear of the Inter City train and never moved out of his seat for the whole six and a half hour journey. He had his earphones attached to his mobile phone and waited. The holdall was in view. All he had to do was get off the train at his stop and return back South and do the same thing but in the opposite direction.

It was easy money. Or so he thought.

Chapter 15

Grace checked her watch. It was 9.10 am. She was unusually late for work this Monday morning and in something of a grumpy mood. She and Tom had been spending quite a bit of time together these last two weeks and Grace felt sure they were heading into a relationship, a personal one. One that involved more than a drink and a kiss.

Why was he being so hard to get?

Hadn't she made it plain enough on more than one occasion that he could take what he wanted. And yet, he was the perfect gentleman. 'Let's keep it professional at work', he'd said, 'But outside of work let's spend more time together'.

That was fine but what Grace actually wanted from Tom was a bit more intimate. She wanted him to spend more time on top of her!

And they had. Spent time together that was. They had eaten out several times, he had come over for supper twice, and last weekend they had gone for a run together. She had managed to keep up, just, which Tom had thought amusing. He pushed her hard, expecting her to cave, but Grace just kept coming back. In the end, they had both fell into each others arms back at hers, exhausted. Yesterday they were due to go running once more but Grace had received a text message very late in the day from Tom who had to cancel feigning illness. His message had been brief and to the point upsetting Grace who was looking forward to their time together.

'Sorry Gracie, feel poorly, can't go running'.

Grace looked at the message in disbelief and texted back immediately.

'Oh dear Tom. Shall I come over? X'.

Grace waited but Tom didn't reply. She waited all afternoon and all evening. Grace picked up her phone a number of times preparing a second text but each time she started pushing the buttons she stopped, eventually deleting the message. Grace had made an effort, reached out, and would not beg. It had put her in a rather grumpy mood this morning though.

As she put her handbag under her work chair, still seething at Tom for his lack of response to her text the day before, her attention was drawn to a bouquet of flowers sat at the side of her desk next to her waste bin. It was the most beautiful arrangement of red roses with a little piece of white gypsophila mixed in. There was a card attached which Grace retrieved.

It read: G. For you. My valentine x

Picking up the flowers which were contained in a very heavy cut glass vase, she placed them pride of place in the middle of her desk. It wasn't often Grace received flowers. In fact, she had never received flowers from anyone as far as she could remember. But today she wanted everyone to see that she too received the occasional gift.

Reading the card once more Grace raised her hand to her mouth.

It was Valentine's Day. 'Oh my god'. She had forgotten.

'Don't worry Gracie, I wasn't expecting flowers', came a whisper in her ear from behind.

Startled, she turned to see Tom smiling at her.

'Don't do that you crazy man. You made me jump'.

'Sorry. And sorry about missing the run yesterday. I just felt off colour'.

'Hmn', replied Grace staring up at him not sure whether he was being truthful or not.

'Can I make it up to you? Tonight, eight, dinner at Romans'.

Grace didn't expect that and was a little shocked at Tom's sudden pushiness.

'Well?', he asked. 'Are we good for tonight, Gracie?'. Tom had taken to calling her Gracie when they were alone.

Nodding, Grace could hardly contain herself long enough to get an answer out but managed a hoarse, 'Yes'.

'Great. I have some clients today so will be out of the office after lunch. I'll meet you at yours at 7.30. Ok?'.

'Yes'.

Tom disappeared back into his office leaving Grace somewhat puzzled at his sudden change. He had emerged from being pursued to being the pursuer. She smiled, logging into her work emails. She wouldn't get much done today, all she had on her mind was Tom.

As Grace slowly ploughed through her work emails, Tom headed out into Mayfair to meet a potential client from the Middle East at a very expensive hotel.

Detective Constable Dave Carter was also hard at work that morning at the BTP HQ in Camden. Like all detectives Dave had a backlog of cases all with bodies attached, live ones that either needed interviewing or arresting. He had been in the office since 10 am trying to catch up on some of his older crime enquiries before Bradshaw answered his bail later that evening. Carter was still struggling with identifying the male in the photograph but had a lead and was hoping the custody sergeant would allow him to extend Archie's bail and give him the extra time he needed.

'Dave', came a voice from the other end of the office. It was the Squad's Detective Inspector, Ellie Scott.

'Ma'am'.

She had a scruffy middle-aged man with her. White male, short in height, maybe 5.9, long grey hair tied in a ponytail, and several days stubble on his face. Carter raised his hand and beckoned the man over. The scruffy bloke held out a hand towards the awaiting Carter.

'DC Douglas Freeman. From Police Scotland's Special Branch based in Glasgow. And call me Doug, please. I hate Douglas'.

'Sure. No problem, Doug. I'm Dave, Dave Carter. I assume you're here about the man in the photograph I sent up to my haggis eating friend. No offence by the way'.

'Aye. It was, and none taken laddie'.

Carter pulled up a chair for the Scotsman and logged into the Bradshaw file.

'So how can I help you, Doug?'.

'I'm hoping we can help each other. Here, let's compare photographs first. Make sure we are talking about the same guy'.

The Scots Detective placed a number of photographs on the desk in front of Carter. All showed what appeared to be the same man but in different locations and dressed in a variety of clothes. But definitely the same man. Carter, in response brought up a set of digital images on the screen in front of him.

'This is what I have Doug. Looks like the same guy who, on the face of it, saved a victim of a serious crime on the London Underground. I've been looking for either him or the victim to support a robbery charge of some description'.

The Scottish DC went quiet as he pondered this information whilst checking his own images against those on the screen.

'Definitely the same man. But…', said the Scotsman.

'But what?', asked Carter.

'Well, we don't think he's a good guy Dave. Not at all. In fact, we believe he is something of a bad guy. And his name we believe may be one Hugo Ross'.

'I doubt it', said Carter, smirking.

'He came to Scotland with a passport in the name of Hugo Ross, but we lost all trace of him shortly after he arrived. He slipped into Scotland by ferry from Belfast and by the time the boys at the port got their act together he was lost somewhere in Glasgow City. We checked everywhere, airports, train stations, bus stations. Nothing'.

Carter was nodding as he scrawled through his digital file.

'Your man here, Hugo Ross yeah. Well, what I can tell you Doug is that he arrived at London City Airport on the 10th November last year from Aberdeen'.

'Aberdeen?'.

'Yeah, Aberdeen. He went North to come south apparently. Here he is at the City Airport'.

Carter brought up an image of Ross passing through passport control.

'I did some checks Doug. Don't know why, but I've got a feeling about this guy. Anyway, I called all the major car hire companies within a ten-mile radius of the airport. I figured that this guy, a businessman maybe, would want to rent a car as soon as possible so I spent the last couple of days on the phone and emailing pictures everywhere of a potential witness to a serious crime'.

'And did ye get anywhere lad'.

'I did indeed Doug. I did indeed. Your man it would appear is Hugo Ross no more. A couple of hours after landing a man matching his description collected a car from the Enterprise car rental booth at Stratford railway terminal, East London. The name on the rental agreement was for a Mr J. Malone. It was really busy at the time and the youngster on the desk accepted payment from what I believe was a pre-paid credit card in that name'.

Carter produced another grainy image and invited Doug to take a good look. The Scot took a good look.

'Could be him, but it's a bit grainy. He has a different coat on. Can't see the suit'.

'Come on Doug. It's him. The briefcase is the same. And the shoes, look'.

'What about the shoes Dave?'.

'The same brown brogues. You can change your coat, put a hat on, specs even. But nobody has time to change their shoes Doug. Come on'.

'It's possible', replied a pensive looking Scotsman.

'There's something else Doug. The rental car, a Ford Focus, was never actually returned. It was reported stolen when it wasn't returned a few days after it should have been and eventually found in a multi storey car park in Croydon three months after it was reported stolen'.

'Fuck'.

'That would be about right Doug. Fuck'.

'What name ye got?'.

'Joseph Malone'.

'I'll be right back', replied the troubled Scotsman, picking up his bag, pictures, coat, and left the office in something of a rush.

He never did come back.

If only he had waited a while longer Dave could have shown him the pictures he had found of the Ford Focus in and around the Kings Cross and Camden area via ANPR, the automatic numberplate recognition system. They were much clearer.

Looking closely at the photographs now it clearly shows the image of a man driving through a red light on the Euston Road at 01.17 am on 6th December. It's a good view of the driver. It's a good view of Hugo Ross, Joseph Malone, or whoever he was.

'Who are you stranger?', whispered Dave Carter to the screen. No answer came back.

The phone on his desk rang. Carter picked up the handset and answered the call before the second ring tone. It was the custody sergeant.

'Hey Sarge. Everything ok'.

There was a short, curt, call from the custody sergeant who had herself just taken a call from an Archie Bradshaw.

'I'll go and collect him sarge', replied Carter.

'You little prick Archie', said a concerned DC Carter heading towards the door.

Chapter 16

Grace took a look at herself in the mirror as she applied the final touch to her makeup. The pink lipstick had a glossy sheen and blended in perfectly with her lilac-coloured Karen Millen dress. A pair of heels completed the look. Not too slutty she thought to herself, but the look was enough to send out the right message, she was sure.

The knock at the door was sharp and unexpected. Grace stood straight and listened. It was 7.28 pm and Tom was due at 7.30. She did have the odd neighbour who knocked but it was unusual. Looking through the spyhole Grace was immediately relieved to see his familiar face.

Tom was a few minutes early when he arrived at Grace's apartment. The cabbie was happy to wait, and Tom gave him a generous tip for doing so. Jogging across the road Tom caught the outer door to Grace's block as a middle-aged woman and younger man left.

'Thank you', Tom responded quickly before rushing up the steps without the need to buzz the apartment. Climbing the steps to Grace's front door he paused momentarily to catch his breath and run his fingers through his hair. Wearing a light grey three-piece Paul Smith wool suit with contrasting pale pink open necked shirt, Tom knew he looked fine but still felt a pang of nerves as he stood outside her front door. Knocking, Tom waited, bringing his breathing back under control. After a slight pause he raised his hand and was about to knock again when the door suddenly opened.

Stood silhouetted by the door frame was the most beautiful woman Tom had ever seen. Grace had scrubbed up better than ever. There was a moment of silence as Tom could not help but stare at the woman in front of him. Grace noticed this, returned the stare, and with a smile appearing in the corner of her mouth she raised an eyebrow at him.

'Tom, you're staring. Stop it'.

'Sorry, I erm…..sorry Grace. Ready'.

'Yes, I am'.

'Then shall we go? The cabbie's waiting'.

The small Italian restaurant was housed down a little-known side street off Regent Street. Roman's had been around for many years and had its regular clientele, well informed Londoners in the main plus the local Italian community who knew good Italian fayre when they saw it. Each customer was welcomed in by the owner himself who appeared to know each and every customer by name. It was no different as Tom opened the door for Grace to enter. Roman arrived from nowhere offering to take their coats and conversing with Tom in perfect Italian.

'Good evening, Mr Ford. Can I get you and your lovely guest an aperitif or some champagne before you take to your table?'.

'Would you like some champagne Grace?', asked Tom.

'Yes, love some, thank you'.

'Some champagne please Roman and perhaps we can take it at our table'.

'Of course, sir. This way please'.

Tom and Grace were led to a small but perfectly placed table towards the rear of the dimly lit restaurant. It was far enough away from the next table to offer enough privacy without feeling isolated. Tom liked it because it offered a good view of the whole place all the way to the entrance. He had visited this restaurant a number of times over the past three months and knew there were exactly ten two-seater tables within the restaurant seating a maximum of twenty people at any one time. Often, tables were merged to make a four or six but tonight all seemed to be small two seaters. Tom noted that they were fully occupied apart from one table but even that one had a reserved sign upon it.

'I didn't know you spoke Italian Tom', said Grace taking a sip of her champagne.

'There's a lot you don't know about me Gracie'.

'Then I'll just have to take some time and find out'.

They both raised and touched their glasses.

A young girl no more than seventeen arrived at their table and asked if they were ready to order. She spoke in English, but Tom replied again in perfect Italian, ordering for both he and Grace. The young waitress smiled at Tom, made a note of the order, and thanked him in Italian for his kind words.

'What was all that about?', asked a surprised Grace, still perusing her own menu.

'I don't know Grace. I, er….just sort of ordered everything for us both. I wasn't thinking, sorry. Shall I call her back?'.

'It's fine Tom. Have you done this before? I mean ordered for someone you are on a date with?'.

Grace was staring at Tom. She didn't mind the fact that she had no choice in ordering the food really. She was quite flattered and thought it quite romantic. His next statement though took her by surprise.

'Thing is Gracie. I don't know who I am'.

'What do you mean. You are a Business Manager, aren't you?'.

Their starters arrived interrupting their conversation flow. Roman placed the food in front of them whilst the young waitress topped their champagne up.

The starter was delicious. Grilled King prawn in a spicy tomato sauce with just a hint of garlic. Grace finished first and was licking her fingers noisily as Tom laughed at her.

'Hungry?', he asked.

'Famished. I've not eaten all day. Just so I can get in this dress. I don't know how I'm going to get out of it'.

Grace realised almost immediately the sexual innuendo from her last statement and her face glowed back at Tom who nearly spat out his final piece of prawn with a coughing fit. They both had a very good idea how Grace was going to get out of her dress later.

'I hope you like to eat meat'.

'Sorry', replied Grace, reddening up once more at Tom's turn at the sexual innuendo.

'Steak. I've ordered us a steak'.

'Just off to the ladies', replied Grace who promptly rose from her chair and headed off in search of the bathroom.

Grace found the bathroom, a small unisex cubicle just off the entrance and applied some more lippy. Things were going well, too well she thought.

Checking her phone, she saw that there were three missed calls from an unknown number. The phone was on silent and there were no unread messages anywhere. Grace did not want any disturbances tonight so in an unusual move for her she switched the mobile phone off, placed it into her bag, and returned to the table.

Tom was sat waiting patiently not checking anything other than her she noticed as she re-joined him at the table. Tom raised his hand towards Roman who came over and both men had a short conversation in Italian. Moments later Grace was looking at her main course.

'Tournedos Rossini', said Tom

'Smells great', replied Grace.

The fillet steak was cooked medium rare, just how Grace liked it, and sat on a fried bread crouton topped with pate and covered in a red wine and mushroom sauce. A few seasonal vegetables were dotted around the plate and a small green salad sat in the middle of the table for them to share. The red Chianti wine completed the main course.

This time Grace took her time. The food was exquisite, and she didn't want to waste any of it. Both devoured their food, and the conversation was put on hold, the food so good neither wanted to miss out on this culinary experience. It gave them both time to think and whilst they talked little over the next fifteen minutes, the body language and eye-catching glances said more than words ever could.

Dabbing the corners of her mouth Grace sat back in the high-backed leather chair and exhaled.

'That was wonderful Tom. But I couldn't eat another thing'.

'They do a great panna cotta'.

'Another time Tom. I need to get out of this dress'.

'Coffee then?'.

'At mine?', asked Grace reddening up once more.

Tom wasted no time in calling Roman over and settling the bill. It took a few minutes in which time there seemed to be an extended conversation in Italian between both men.

When Tom returned from settling up he reached out for Grace's hand and helped her from her chair.

'Taxi's outside. Shall we'.

'Yes please', said Grace, their eyes meeting with an intensity.

Twenty minutes later Tom had no sooner walked through the door to Grace's apartment when she flung her arms around him and kissed him, passionately. Tom found himself responding, gently at first, then with more probing and passion.

Grace found it was a lot easier to get out of the dress than it was to get into and withing ten minutes of arriving at her apartment Grace Canning gave herself completely to this stranger called Tom Ford.

They made love twice that night before succumbing to a deep sleep in each other's arms, then a third time in the morning before they both headed into work together. Exhausted.

Chapter 17

March 1st

Grace is awakened by a whistling sound coming from her kitchen. She smiles to herself knowing that the man in her kitchen is happy. He whistles when he's happy. It's been four days and three nights since they slept in different beds and Grace loved it. She didn't like the 'L' word, but she was definitely falling for this man. Reaching under the bed she fumbled around until the book was in her hand. Blowing off the dust and making a mental note to herself, 'I must hoover more', Grace turned to the next page and started to write in her diary.

'I am exhausted once again. But in a good way. He likes me on top and I love to be in control. Mum, if you ever read this, please stop, NOW! Anyway, we are an item, I think. I'm getting to know Tom, the real Tom, although he sometimes frightens me by how resourceful he is, and not just in the bedroom, LOL'.

Grace draws a smiling face and is about to continue but is interrupted by a naked man carrying a tray.

'Breakfast is served madame'.

Placing the tray on the bed beside Grace, Tom proudly displays the freshly brewed coffee and pancakes covered in maple syrup.

'Let's eat them later', whispered Grace, pushing the tray aside and sliding out of the bed.

'But they're delicious', protested Tom, now looking down at Grace in all her nakedness sat in front of him.

'Not as delicious as you are', said Grace with a naughty giggle. Pulling Tom forward Grace Canning decided that the first thing she ate this morning would not be a pancake. Tom threw his head back, gasping at the pleasure he was experiencing from the woman in front of him.

Fifteen minutes later Grace put the final piece of pancake into her mouth.

'Hey, that was great. Where'd you learn that?'

'I don't know. Where did you learn to do that?', replied Tom.

'No comment'

They both laughed.

'So, what shall we do for the rest of the day Mr Ford?'.

Grace picked up the tray from the bed and took it over to the kitchen work top. Glancing over at Tom she watched his expression change and could tell he was thinking, making a plan. He had this way of turning his eyes upwards towards the heavens as he was about to come out with something.

'It's St David's day today, Gracie. Did you know that?'.

'No. who is he?'.

'The patron saint of Wales'.

'So'.

'So, I'm thinking. Let's go to Wales'.

Grace was a little confused by his suggestion. Resting her chin on her hands and looking back at Tom she spoke in a decidedly unconvincing manner.

'You want to go to Wales. The country Wales?'.

'I do'.

'Why?'.

'I don't know. Come on. Get dressed'.

It is late afternoon when Tom and Gracie walk into the George Hotel in the middle of Brecon Town centre. A Georgian hotel, it is a favourite of tourists and military families alike visiting the area.

Grace watched as Tom booked them a room. He seemed to know his way around the place. Grace watched the receptionist closely as she appeared to smile and converse with him as if he was a regular customer. The body language between them was friendly and not at all formal. Grace watched and studied her more closely. A middle-aged woman, not unattractive, she wore her greying hair tied up giving her a professional look to go with the uninspiring brown two-piece suit she wore. Grace was sure she heard her speak in Welsh and Tom replying before they both reverted to English, although from where Grace was sat a short distance away on a small sofa in the foyer, she couldn't quite make out much of the conversation. She did find it interesting to see the woman offer Tom two different keys and Tom deliberating with her over which one to choose. Perhaps she was offering him a choice. Strange thing was though, he shook his head, said something else about room seven and with a smile the receptionist reached under the desk and produced a third key which he then accepted.

Grace turned away sharply when Tom came over. She didn't want him to know she had been watching him so carefully. Deep down, she didn't know why but she felt she should. Grace couldn't explain it. It was just how she felt.

'Room number seven', said Tom. 'It's one of the best'.

'Really, how do you know?'.

This seemed to stop Tom in his tracks.

He stood there, quietly pondering this question and looked down at the key fob, a small three-inch wooded block with the number seven imprinted upon it.

'I erm..I don't know Grace actually'.

'Have you brought someone else here Mr Ford?'.

Grace had a smile on her face and gave Tom a teasing look, crossing her arms and sitting back on the sofa. Tom seemed visibly shaken by the question and his face drained of all colour. Grace became concerned, stood up and approached him.

'I'm just kidding Tom. It's a lovely place. Let's unpack and go explore the town'.

Grace took Tom's arm and led him towards the stairs. A sign at the bottom was displayed which read: 'ROOMS 1-7'.

'I bet we are on the top floor', said Grace as she lifted her overnight bag and slung it over her shoulder.

'We are', replied Tom, doing the same with his own bag and following behind Grace as she set off up the staircase.

Brecon is a relatively small town in South Wales with a population of around 8,500 inhabitants. And of those inhabitants a large portion have some connection to the British military. Soldiers are a regular sight in and around the town and the Brecon Beacons are renowned for their connection to the SAS, it's terrain a particularly testing environment for even the best infantry units.

Tom Ford was comfortable in this town. He knew it well.

After three wonderful days, and two exhausting nights, Grace and Tom reluctantly returned to London. Driving through the Welsh countryside both are lost in their own thoughts. Wishing for different worlds with less responsibility, less stress, less violence. Grace eventually broke the silence.

'I love this place. So peaceful. I wish we could stay longer'.

'Yeah. Me too Gracie'.

'Why don't we then?'.

'Work for one'.

'I could get a job somewhere. I have plenty of transferable skills Tom'.

Tom looked over at Grace, now sat up and looking at him as he drove. She seemed to be serious about this.

Grace was serious. She liked the remoteness of the Brecon Beacons, of this part of Wales. It was somewhere they could both get lost in.

Tom momentarily looked over at Grace then back towards the open road ahead. A sign indicated 23 miles to Cardiff. Grace was not finished yet and went on with her proposal.

'This feels right Tom. I have some money tucked away to keep us going for a while. Quite a while actually. And I'm sure you could get a job in the town, or the city maybe. Cardiff is not that far, and....'.

'Grace', interrupted Tom.

Grace went quiet. Waiting for him to go on.

'Well?', she asked.

'I just can't at the moment. We can't just up and leave London Grace. Not yet anyway. I still don't know enough about myself Grace'.

Grace turned to face the road ahead and slumped back in the car seat. After several minutes of silence and resigned to facing life in London for at least a while longer she reached over and gently stroked Tom's leg. Tom smiled and spoke again in a strong Welsh accent causing Grace to laugh out loud.

'Are you making this up or do you really have a local accent?'.

Tom laughed back. 'I don't really know. It does seem to come naturally'.

'And who were those men that spoke to you in the pub last night?'.

'I don't know. I think they were just being really friendly'.

'Hmn..', Grace wasn't sure. 'They seemed over friendly to me'.

'Just drunk that's all. The Welsh are like that'. Tom raised his Welsh accent to another level.

'Were they soldiers Tom?'.

'Why do you ask?'.

'Just interested. They all had short hair, fit looking, and one of them addressed you as Sir'.

'Did he? I never noticed'.

'Do you think you may have been in the Army Tom?'.

Nodding as he drove, 'It's possible I suppose'.

Grace left the questioning there and let Tom continue his drive. They were approaching the M4 motorway and Tom took the Eastbound direction towards London. Grace settled back into the comfortable leather seat and closed her eyes.

As Grace slept Tom recalled the previous evening in the Fox and Hounds Pub. The men that approached him. Men he did in fact recognise. His thoughts drifted back to a faraway place, a violent place, a team of soldiers led by a young officer.

Chapter 18

Afghanistan, 10 years earlier

'Stand up', yelled the squad sergeant as the young man walked into the briefing hut at Basra.

The young officer shouted back towards the four soldiers who were slowly dragging their chairs back.

'Sit for Fuck sake boys', replied the tanned young man pulling a chair up to the small table.

'Righto, I'm new and this is my first op so please let me know if I'm fucking things up'.

The four men all nodded and one, a thick set man in his late thirties, cheekily replied, 'We will sir, don't worry'.

'Don't be bloody insolent Smithy'.

'Sorry Sarge, but he did ask'.

'It's Lieutenant or Sir, not he'.

The two squaddies stood and started to square up with each other.

This is ridiculous thought the young officer.

'Fucking hell boys. They said you were a difficult team but I'm not fucking going in if you're like this. Call me Brandon, not Sir, and definitely not Taffy. Right. And fucking sit down'.

The two soldiers sat and gave each other a high five. This was just a bit of a test for their young new officer. He had passed the first one.

The blue team had been waiting for the call for weeks and were on the verge of giving up all hope, fully expecting a recall to Hereford when their last team leader had broken his leg on exercises. But things were looking up as a new 'Rupert' had been put in place.

'Okay, listen up', said 25-year-old Lieutenant Brandon Lewis.

'We are going in tonight. It's a hostage recovery op deep into the hills. The chopper will drop us five clicks out in cover of darkness. There is just one hostage being held by Taliban resistance fighters. We don't know how many fighters there are. We are to go in, assess the situation, and decide on the spot whether the hostage recovery is doable. If it is, we go in. If not, we retrace our steps and evac by foot to the RV point'.

South Wales, Eight years earlier.

Seventeen-year-old Brandon Lewis walked into the Army recruitment office on Cardiff's St Mary's Street on a cold, wet, January morning. An only child to Margaret and Jeffrey Lewis, both Civil Servants, he had taken the news of their death all too well from his house master at the Monmouth School where he was a weekly boarder whilst his parents spent most of their week working in London. The car had skidded on a patch of ice he had been told; control had been lost. His father had crashed through the carriageway barrier on the A40 flyover bridge, landing on the carriageway, some twenty meters below. Both parents were killed instantly.

Brandon accepted the news with unusual aplomb. There were no tears. He packed his bags and left school immediately, returning to the family home in the Llandaff area of Cardiff.

December had been the worst month in his young life thus far. Parents killed on the 16th, a funeral on the 29th, he was alone, frustrated, and angry. A man from the Home Office had come to visit the day after the accident. The man, a colleague of his deceased parents he had said, told Lewis many financial facts about pensions, mortgages, insurance schemes, but very little about his actual parents. By the time the man had left it was clear that Brandon was financially ok but mentally on the edge. Not allowed to visit his deceased mother and father, all funeral arrangements were made for him, and at the funeral itself, only Brandon, the man from the Home Office, and the local vicar were in attendance. As both coffins were lowered into the ground the vicar said his final prayer and Brandon Lewis was struck by the fact that he was now all alone in the world. He had no one. Absolutely no one.

The man from the Home Office turned towards Brandon as the rain started to slowly fall.

He was about to say something, but Brandon spoke first.

'Now what do I do?'.

'Two choices son. Go back to school would be my advice. Get an education'.

The man started to walk away but stopped as Brandon called after him.

'The second choice. What is it?'.

'Join the Army son. That's what I did'.

The following week Brandon Lewis took the second option. He joined the Army. In particular, The Welsh Guards. Their regiment was in need of local talent, so the recruiting sergeant had said, and Brandon Lewis signed up straight away. There was a basic training course in Aldershot due to start in three weeks. The recruiting sergeant helped Lewis through the application procedure, arranged for him to attend a fitness test in Aldershot, which he sailed through, and a short notice recruitment interview with the Section

Commander, an Army Captain, who needed to sign off the application to add his name to the list with the other forty-five recruits.

The Army Captain, a veteran of the Falklands conflict noticed Lewis recent family tragedy. He also noticed his academic prowess. Brandon Lewis had accumulated eleven 'O' levels, all either A or A*, three of which were in foreign languages, French, Italian, and German.

'You know Brandon, with these qualifications you could apply for Officer training. It would mean more testing, a visit to Westbury, and a wider choice of regiment. There is an officer training course due to start in June'.

'Anything sooner Sir?'.

'Just junior infantry training in three weeks'.

'Then I'd like to sign up for that, please'.

Captain Stoddart looked directly into the eyes of the young man in front of him. He could see a need in those eyes. He was looking at a lonely young man who needed to belong, be a part of a family. He had lost one family and now needed another. The Army could give him that family.

'Welcome to the Welsh guards Brandon Lewis'.

The officer stood and stretched out his hand. Brandon took the proffered hand and said, 'Thank you sir'.

The Army Captain retrieved an envelope from his desk drawer and handed it to Brandon.

'Everything you need is in here. Instructions on where to report, what to bring with you, and one single railway ticket. Good luck'.

Brandon nodded, turned, and left the office of this Army veteran and headed straight back to Llandaff. He needed to do some research on the Welsh guards, their traditions, and most importantly, their training programme.

Captain Stoddart watched the young man as he left. There was something about this one. A vulnerability mixed with strength. Stoddart opened the file in front of him and inserted a note in red in a section on the back page left free for the recruiting officer to make any comment they liked about the candidate.

Stoddart wrote the following:

'This boy is one to watch. Definitely Officer material and potentially one for the Foreign Office later on'.

He picked up the phone and placed a call through to Aldershot.

'Martin. It's James Stoddart here from the RO in Cardiff. I've got a late one for you. A young man, Brandon Lewis. I expect him to do well. Keep me informed would you'.

Three weeks later Private Brandon Lewis stood on the parade ground at Aldershot, his first official day of training.

Twelve weeks later he stood there once again passing out as best student after excelling at all aspects of Army life.

An excellent shot with every piece of weaponry put in front of him, Lewis took to Army life immediately. The physicality of the training suited him, and he found that he was good at running, particularly cross country, and came away with the 10 K cross country record at Aldershot. No mean feat for a now eighteen-year-old.

Self-defence training was a breeze, and he could hold his own against any of the other recruits, most of whom were older, heavier, but a lot less clever. Lewis used his brain where many of his peers could not. This did not go unnoticed by the training staff who had no problem with awarding him the top student award. This was followed by an extra three-week sniper training course in the Brecon

Beacons followed by a two-week parachute training course in Lympstone, Devon. By the time Lewis joined the Welsh Guards Regiment in mid-May they were about to be deployed to Bosnia as part of a peacekeeping force.

Going from strength-to-strength Lewis acquitted himself well during his first few weeks in Bosnia, witnessing many atrocities between the warring Serbs and Croats. His troop Sergeant quickly acknowledged that they had a young diamond within their team. He most certainly had an old head on young shoulders and when a small team of patrolling guardsmen of whom Lewis was one came under fire becoming cut off from the rest of their platoon it was Lewis who took control of the situation when their section leader took a direct hit to the head and died instantly. It was an unexpected attack on a peacekeeping force. A war crime.

'Fuck, fuck, fuck', screamed a young guardsman as he hit the ground taking cover.

'What the fuck are we gonna do now boys', replied the oldest of the three, also taking cover. The whistling sound of 7.62mm rounds tracing past their heads could clearly be heard.

Brandon Lewis, who had been close enough to the dead section leader to see where the shot had come from, was on one knee, rifle raised, returning fire in two shot bursts. The body of his dead colleague was in front of him and being used for cover. It was the most sensible thing to do at the time if he was to stay alive.

Unclipping the section leaders' radio and throwing it over to the other two guardsmen Lewis spoke in an authoritative manner.

'Jenkins, start fucking shooting. My ten o'clock. Wilson, call in our position then start shooting. We fight back'.

And fight back they did.

The three Welsh guardsmen all received bravery awards for their actions that day. A dissident Serbian group had apparently stumbled across the small team and decided to take pot shots at the British peacekeepers. It was a mistake. They had one kill, Lewis, Jenkins, and Wilson had sixteen. There were no Serbian survivors and the whole contact lasted a little over eight minutes.

Nothing was ever reported in the press other than to say a small team had behaved with honour when coming under fire. The dead guardsman was given the DSO, distinguished service order, Lewis, the Military Medal, and the other two were mentioned in dispatches.

Back at camp there was a thorough de-brief of all three surviving soldiers.

All gave similar accounts to coming under fire, losing their leader, and retaliating as per the Geneva convention. The Army top brass were duly impressed by the soldiers, particularly the actions of the youngest guardsman Lewis, who used a total of one hundred and forty rounds of ammunition compared to his colleagues who used a total of thirty-nine between them.

Lewis and his Welsh Guards colleagues returned from their 3-month tour of Bosnia without further incident, much to Lewis' disappointment. But he did return to Aldershot with two stripes on his arm. It was Corporal Lewis, but only for a few weeks.

After a visit from the base commander one Monday morning in December, almost a year after joining the Army, Lewis was once again being encouraged to put pen to paper. An officer training course was due to begin late January and they were looking for soldiers who could lead under fire. Lewis, it was felt, was one of those. The application was submitted that same day and following a successful assessment at the Officer Assessment Centre later that month Lewis began Officer training exactly one year and a day after starting his basic Army training.

The 'Sword of Honour' followed as 2nd Lieutenant Lewis once more came out as top student. After graduating from officer training, he took up an option to switch regiments and decided that his best chance of further action came with the Royal Marines.

Brandon Lewis turned twenty years old whilst cruising through the long commando course in Devon before joining his unit.

The young officer returned to his unit as a platoon commander and as he had secretly hoped, was quickly deployed to Helmand Province in Afghanistan.

A commando, trained sniper, and decorated soldier, Lewis quickly came to notice once more with the Army top brass. There was much contact between the British Forces and the insurgents in Afghanistan but whereas most allied forces retreated and took cover when under fire, the British, and particularly those led by 2nd Lieutenant Lewis, did not. They took the fight right back to the enemy.

After one long and uneventful foot patrol, Lewis stood his men down and discarded his kit. He was not tired and would run off his excess energy. Just as he was about to run the perimeter of the camp a chopper landed in the drop zone.

A special forces soldier jumped out and came running over.

'Hey soldier. We need an extra rifle to back us up. Quick mission. Any idea who we can call on'.

'Yeah, me'.

'Nah, you're a bit young son. We need a sniper. Someone who can shoot'.

'That's me mate. Yes or no cos if it's no I'm off for a run'.

'Hurry up', came the shout from the chopper.

The soldier from the chopper thought for a moment then checked his watch. Lewis noted his black protective gear had no rank insignia on or any sort of regimental badge. The hair and facial stubble gave it all away. Brandon knew who this soldier's regiment was.

'Ok, you're on'.

'I'll get my kit', said Lewis.

'No need. Just get in. Use ours'.

It was unusual for Special Forces to take on board unvetted personnel, but this was a one off. They were a man down and needed an extra rifle for cover.

As darkness fell the chopper dropped the team off in a clearing with some tree cover. They were in rural Afghanistan. Farmland. Poppies. Drug production.

Lewis was kitted up with a protective vest, night goggles, and a state-of-the-art American made sniper rifle with full mag plus spare.

'Ok son. You and Jackson here are our protection. You each take up a covering position. When you hear the explosions, you watch. Shoot anything that threatens the chopper or is giving chase. Understand?'.

'Yes', replied Lewis.

'Yep', replied Jackson.

'Just don't shoot us lads', grinned the black clad soldier.

Lewis and Jackson set themselves up with their rifles about 200 meters north and south of the stationary chopper with a view of the tree line. Lewis locked and loaded the US Army Remington model 700 snipers' rifle and stared down the scope. Switching the safety to off he waited, constantly scanning the area. The night vision goggles magnetically attached themselves to the scope as the eye piece closed in. Lewis was in the lying prone position, rifle poised upon its tripod. After eight long minutes Lewis heard the first explosion. It was quickly followed by a second, then a third. Small arms fire quickly followed the explosions.

Looking down the night scope Lewis placed the cross hairs upon his first target. A non-military male dressed in white robe and flowing headgear appeared on the edge of the tree line carrying what Lewis knew was a Russian AK 47. A second male soon followed, both carrying automatic rifles. Lewis fired and his first target fell. The second male soon followed and fell to the ground following a second and third round fired from Lewis' suppressed rifle. More small arms fire, closer now, and the two special forces guys came into view. They ran in tag style, one stopped, crouched and returned fire whilst the other ran back towards the chopper.

More warriors in white appeared from the trees and fired wildly. Lewis and Jackson went to work with renewed vigour. It was easy pickings for the young Lewis who fired with 100% accuracy. Each shot hit its target and the two special ops guys quickly reached the chopper. An instruction to run towards the chopper for an evac was initially ignored by Lewis as he took aim at one more pursuing non friendly. The sight of the shoulder held anti-aircraft weapon caused Lewis to drop to his knee whilst in fast evac mode and raise the rifle one more time. A quick three shot burst took out the unfriendly who dropped the weapon. A fourth shot impacted with the anti-aircraft weapon and the ensuing explosion gave Lewis the time he needed to hot foot it to the chopper reaching the bird just as it was ready to take off.

 Jackson took Lewis by his arm and yanked him on board before firing rapidly into the darkness below.

When they were airborne and out of range of their pursuers Jackson slapped Lewis on the shoulder.

'Fuck me son. That was some shooting. What regiment are you in?'.

'The Marines, 42 commando, close combat troop'.

'We'll have a word with your platoon leader. What's his name?'.

'Lewis, 2nd Lieutenant Lewis'.

'What's your name son?', screamed Jackson, finding it difficult to communicate over the noise of the rotors.

'Lewis. 2nd Lieutenant Brandon Lewis'.

Chapter 19

Afghanistan, Eight years later.

Lewis led the four-man team deep into rural Afghanistan under cover of darkness. A stealth chopper flying as low as possible had dropped the team five clicks away from the target and now, after a two-hour power march, the target was in view. To an uninformed onlooker the smallholding up ahead was just a simple farmstead. A few goats, some poultry, and the small tin roofed habitable shack was not much to look at. But the armed men constantly patrolling its perimeter indicated otherwise.

This was it. Game on.

They had gone through the plan time and time again until all were clear what was expected. The single hostage should be inside the shed and would be instantly recognised. He was to be liberated and taken back to the RV point for evacuation at all costs.

Smithy set up position on an elevated section of ground with an unobstructed view of the front of the target area. Instructions were clear. Wait for Lewis' signal then take out as many of the patrolling enemy. Lewis, Cooper, and Maguire would do the rest.

It took a good hour for Lewis and his men to crawl their way towards the target. At fifty meters out Lewis stopped and took in the scene. It was somewhere around 3 am, a good time to strike. The sky was clear and gave the team a good view of what was ahead of them. Unfortunately, it also gave the hostage takers a good all-round view of the surrounding area. Another slow 25 meters and Lewis found himself face to face with a goat. The thin wire fence was just a token to keep the animals in. It would not keep anyone else out. The hand signal given saw Cooper peel off left whilst Maguire quickly clipped the wire.

Movement now, two patrolling enemy appeared. The clear sky should have enabled them to spot the rescue team, but a combination of fatigue given the hour, and the totally unexpected situation meant that they virtually walked over the bodies of Lewis and Maguire. Lewis raised a hand to the vertical and quickly dropped it back towards the ground. The two patrolling men dropped immediately, taken out by a two-shot burst from Smithy. Up and moving at pace Lewis quickly reached the wooden outer door to the shack. Muffled sounds from nearby told the young officer that Cooper had dispatched the other two external guards. This was confirmed seconds later as he re appeared alongside Lewis, gave a nod, and held up four fingers. The chopping motion across his throat confirmed four dead.

Another hand signal from Lewis to Maguire and it was a go.

The thunder flash exploded within two seconds of its entry into the shed. Cooper kicked in the door shortly after Maguire had hurled in the flash and the explosion rang out. The three-man team had entered almost immediately, protected by ear defenders and wearing night vision glasses.

'Stay down or die', came the shout from Maguire.

Movement from their right caused a burst of suppressed fire from Lewis, who took out a Taliban fighter holding an AK 47. A second enemy fighter sat at the table was quickly dispatched by Cooper. A third, unfortunately, was crouched in the opposite corner and held a knife to the throat of the hostage.

The ginger haired hostage seemed to be unharmed, if a little shocked at the intrusion, but was now clearly fearful for his life. Dressed in army fatigues, he had looked better. Particularly when stood alongside other members of the Royal family on parades, but at this moment those occasions were a million miles away. Now, at this moment, his life was at risk. The Taliban fighter holding the knife opened his mouth to speak but before any words came out his head snapped back, a red mist exploding all over the hostage.

Lewis signalled to the two troopers who proceeded to check outside then gave the all-clear. It was time to leave. Lewis moved towards the hostage who was not moving.

'We have to go, now'.

The ginger hostage seemed to snap out of his shocked situation, understanding suddenly dawning upon him. He turned to his left and vomited.

'Sir, we have to go', came a voice from the door. Cooper had returned and was beckoning both the hostage and the officer to leave.

Lewis gave his instruction and took a crouched position outside. Cooper followed, dragging a subdued ginger hostage as he went. There was no crawling back. Lewis and Maguire took it in turns to give cover whilst Cooper and the recovered hostage made their way towards Smithy.

Smithy remained in place watching the farmstead for another 30 minutes whilst the others hot yomped to the evac point.

The demeanour of the ginger hostage improved as they went and by the time they reached the evac point three hours later he was fully in control of himself and very ungrateful. As the evac chopper landed the hostage turned to Cooper.

'Who's fucking in charge here. I was nearly killed out there. I want your names and regiment'.

Cooper looked at Lewis who shook his head.

The ginger whinger continued, now turning his attention to Lewis.

'Do you know who I am?'.

The movement was swift and brought the one-way conversation to an abrupt end.

Smithy, not the most up to date on current affairs did not like the way this ungrateful twat was behaving and decked him with a short but very sharp jab to the chin, knocking him out instantly.

Bundling him into the chopper the team travelled back to base in silence. As the team left the chopper it quickly took off again and headed back to the safe compound at Basra from where the hostage would be repatriated to the UK.

He would never find out who his rescuers were.

Chapter 20

London, Present day.

As Tom and Grace drove along roads that skirted the Severn estuary on their way back from the George Hotel in Brecon, both were deep in thought, miles away, reliving moments from their past.

Whilst they drove in silence, a meeting was taking place on the Thames estuary riverboat one hundred and seventy-eight miles away.

Three men had boarded at three different stops along the route from Westminster on the Thames riverboat and were now sat on an exposed bench at the rear. All three wore long trench coats, collars pulled up at an attempt to fend off the bitterly cold wind that seemed to blow along the Thames no matter what time of year it was. They were sat alone and some distance away from any other passengers. They were not accustomed to the ways of statecraft and their attempts at anonymity were only successful in their own minds. Two of the men were senior ranks within their governmental departments and usually employed others to undertake this type of clandestine meeting. The third man was more accustomed to the ways and was only present due to his lower position in the establishment food chain.

'Well, Mr Collins. Do you bring us good news?', asked the one man who wore a hat.

'Please sir, no names. It's in all our interests to refrain from any form of identification'.

'Get on with it man. Fanshawe and I have to get back to the office. Is there a problem or not?'.

Patrick Collins, a forty-five-year-old veteran of clandestine government operations, sighed to himself. The men in front of him were liabilities and well out of their depths when it came to tradecraft. Unfortunately, they were decision makers. And sometimes they made decisions which cost people their lives.

'For the greater good', was their comeback statement. Collins had spent ten years in British Army Intelligence before being recruited by the security services. In the last twelve years he had shown himself to be a resourceful individual with a knack of getting things done. A problem solver. A tactician. An expert in many fields.

A killer.

He was no James Bond and was not privy to the bigger picture. He generally had orders to watch and report back, sometimes to eliminate a foreign threat, but this recent operation was causing him some deep concern. He knew all governments were not as squeaky clean as they maintained. Often selling arms to dubious countries with terrible human rights records, knowing full well those arms would likely be used against some of our allies. Giving haven to dirty money from all over the world, allowing free passage to foreign despots, particularly Russian and Middle Eastern. He knew all this. But this most recent operation where the state seems to have sanctioned and become part of organised crime within the UK had hit him hard. He was struggling with it, and his particular role within it.

'The supply route is up and running sir, yes. It seems to be working well enough', reported Collins.

'Any problems with local law enforcement?'.

'Not really. No seizures as yet and not likely'.

The two men sat opposite Collins were nodding.

'The money?', questioned Mr Fanshawe.

'It's all being delivered to the location you have told me to deliver it to, twice weekly, sometimes three. Each time one bag is dropped off'.

'Good', replied Fanshawe.

The trench coated man with the hat leaned closer into Collins.

'This is drug money that would otherwise go to organised crime. We are just routing it back into society. To causes that will help our drug and crime problem in the long run. Trust us. You are doing good here Mr Collins'.

Fanshawe rose and spoke at the same time.

'Five million pounds each drop. That's fifty million plus each month. Six hundred million a year to help bolster our health service, schools, police. They all need paying for. This is a tax on crime Collins'.

And with that Fanshawe gave him a condescending pat on the shoulder and walked off the boat.

'We'll be in touch', said the second man as he too followed Fanshawe off the boat and out towards the Cutty Sark ship and Greenwich village.

Chapter 21

London, Oxford Street

The John Lewis store was busy.

DC Dave Carter was in need of help, and he felt this was the best place to get it. Pushing through the crowds of customers he wondered if the store was always this busy. The red signs hanging above the perfumery counter gave him the answer. Not only was it Saturday, but it was also offering '50% reduction today only'.

Carter had been in the doghouse all week and needed to make an effort with her indoors. He had become obsessed with this latest case and knew he had some serious making up to do. Beckoning the female assistant over he had to raise his voice to be heard.

'Excuse me. Can you help me'.

The female assistant, a woman similar in age to his own wife, came over sensing a sale or two and smiled.

'I'm desperate and need advice. What do you have that is new?', asked Carter.

The woman smiled a knowing smile then reached under the counter and placed a number of boxes on the counter top in front of Carter. She also started spraying perfume on small pieces of card which she placed under his nose.

Carter felt hot and bothered. It was so claustrophobic in the store; he could hardly breathe. Packed with customers and a hundred different smells in the air. It was stifling.

Truth was that all the cards smelled the same.

A confused Carter checked his watch. It was 4pm already and he had promised Mrs C he would be home by five. Now he was struggling to make a decision.

'Which would you choose?', he asked the assistant, stood there in front of him, arms crossed, smirking. She knew exactly what was going on. She saw it every day. Men looking to make up to their women with perfume.

She picked up the box on the far left and said, 'This one'.

'It's very new and called Black Opium. So intense, sensual. I love it'. She was looking directly into Carter's eyes.

'I'll take it', replied Carter breaking away from her intense stare.

After paying in cash the assistant handed over the perfume, now gift wrapped, and asked, 'Anything else?'.

There was a cheeky look in her eye. Carter felt like she was flirting and if he wasn't already taken he would be flattered. But as it was, it was a no no.

'No thank.....what are these?'. Carter had seen something.

Carter was about to leave when he caught sight of a number of other boxes of perfume placed on the shelves behind the counter.

'These are for men. Also, on offer', said the assistant sensing another potential sale.

Carter was looking at a range of men's cologne.

Hugo Boss, Calvin Klein, Tom Ford. All names that he had heard before but not until now did they mean anything to him.

'This is my favourite, Jo Malone', interrupted the assistant.

Carter looked up at her.

'Sorry. What did you call it?'.

'Jo Malone. I think it would suit you'.

Carter didn't hear the last bit. He was off, pushing through the crowds once more. He never heard the next call from the assistant either.

'Hey, your perfume. Sir, your perfume'.

Too late. Carter was gone, Mrs C's gift left with the open-mouthed assistant. He never went home. Instead, he headed back to the CID office. He needed to get the Bradshaw file out. A name was bugging him. All thoughts of perfume and Mrs C gone, Carter would not get back to his home for another 24 hours by which time his wardrobe would be half empty. Mrs C, long gone.

Chapter 22

Collins watched the CCTV recording once again. The picture was not perfect but clear enough. Recognition was instant. Collins turned towards Carter with an intense look.

'Where did you get this recording Detective?'.

'You spooks are so fucking dumb. I'm a detective. Where do you think I got it from?'.

The blow to the back of the head sent Carter sprawling and unconscious. He was on his knees with his hands tied behind his back with plastic ties when he finally opened his eyes and recovered himself. The cold water causing him to swear.

After leaving the John Lewis store last week Carter had rushed back to the office. Flipping through the intel reports and the Bradshaw statements he knew he had seen the name before. But where?

The Bradshaw file was thick, and it took Carter a good hour to get through, but no name stuck out that caused Carter to raise his head.

Recent intel reports next, with the same result. The last report was from Police Scotland linking a wanted male by their SB to what they describe as an as yet unidentified OCG, organised crime group. And there it was. On the last page of the last report.

Joseph Malone.

A name linked to a stolen hire vehicle, a man arriving in London's City airport from Jock land, and CCTV images connecting that same individual to a man on the underground. A man he was looking for. But Joseph Malone didn't exist. It was an alias.

A google search of the ten most popular men's fragrances gave Carter a list of names. A few tweaks gave him another twenty and a total of thirty plus names to start researching. He was sure that one of the names on this list was going to lead him to the mysterious male in the CCTV.

Collins banged on the internal panel and the vehicle set off once more. Closing the briefcase, he nodded to the two men who lifted Carter and sat him up. He was still dazed from the head blow but was quickly brought back by a bottle of cold water being poured over his head.

'Oh, fuck. Fuck off. Stop'.

The vehicle came to a halt and the side panel door opened. Carter was dragged over to the open door and held by the two thugs who had bundled him into the vehicle over two hours previously.

'Detective. One last chance. Who is this man in the photographs you have? Tell me now to save your life'.

Carter was staring out at the waters of the Thames some fifty feet below. The vehicle was stationary on Vauxhall bridge and the drop below would surely finish the detective, particularly with hands secured.

'I've no fucking idea. Not yet anyway, you fucking maniacs', screamed Carter.

Collins nodded and one of the two men holding the detective gave him a push in the back.

'We'll be in touch', called the man closing the door as the vehicle sped away.

Carter landed with a thud on the side of the road inches away from the barrier. As he watched the white transit drive off at speed, he attempted to pick out the registration number but knew it would be a fruitless task. The number, if it existed at all, would most likely be blocked or stolen. The first four digits were all that he managed, his vision being momentarily disturbed by the picture of a black briefcase flying through the air and into the Thames below. His briefcase.

'Fuck'.

Chapter 23

Grace reached over and picked up the ringing phone. She took the call, initially sitting up and trying not to disturb Tom, but when she heard the voice on the other end, she quickly left the comfort of her bed and made her way into the bathroom, the only place where she would be guaranteed some privacy.

'Yes', replied Grace in response to the caller's question. This was followed by two further one-word responses, both 'Yes', after which the call was terminated, and she quietly crept back into bed. The warmth of the bed was comforting and fortunately for Grace, Tom had not moved an inch even as she slowly slipped back under the covers. It was still dark, the bedside clock read 3.45 am. Nestling her body into Tom he responded with a little groan before pulling her in closer. His breathing was steady and deep with a regular rhythmic pattern. Fast asleep. Grace tried to relax but her heart was pounding. The caller was adamant. She was to facilitate a further exchange, today. And terminate the courier.

Tom felt movement. He was a light sleeper, always had been. He knew Grace had left the bed and was about to speak when he heard the low-pitched sound of the phone ringing. As Grace left the bed to take the call Tom noted the time and waited. Who was calling her at this hour? They spent most of their spare time together now and much of their work time. Tom felt comfortable in her presence. Safe somehow. He lay in wait and decided to stay put. Grace returned quickly to their bed and snuggled back into him. Tom pulled her in closer. Whoever had called had been brief and it couldn't have been urgent as she was back in his arms. Tom had his own breathing under control but felt Grace's heart pounding. He left his arm in place and it took a good three or four minutes before her heart rate returned to a normal level. Tom made a mental note and went back to sleep.

Chapter 24

Brick Lane, London

Archie Bradshaw was back on the gear. He had given in one evening after one of his recent lucrative courier gigs had brought him in an excessive amount of cash. Bradshaw had been given strict instructions by his contact.

'Collect, Drop, Collect, Drop'.

Bradshaw had nodded his understanding but the crushing hand around his throat had been a firm reminder of what would happen if he fucked up.

'Do not open the bags. Understand?', came the brutal instruction from his contact.

It was all he could do to nod his head in the affirmative.

The accent was British, but not Southern. It had a twang to it. Maybe Geordie, he wasn't sure. Either way, Bradshaw had got the gig he wanted but he needed to keep off drugs, keep his head down, and he would earn £500 for each drop. Easy money.

But Archie Bradshaw was greedy. He was a thief and a junkie. It was a matter of time before he fell off the drugs wagon or opened the bag. As it turned out, he did both. There was so much money in the bag he couldn't resist. Just a few £50's off the top of a few bundles was gonna double his take. Nobody would miss a few hundred from millions surely.

But they did.

Walking along Brick Lane, Bradshaw perused the market stalls looking for the one that would spell payday. Artisan food and craft stalls were in abundance this morning, but it was a second-hand bag stall that Archie was looking for. As is typical with this type of market stall it was not always in the same place. Today, the stall was housed behind a very bohemian looking fabric stall and next to one selling dog baskets and pet clothing. There was the same old woman on the stall that Archie had seen each and every one of his six visits so far. He didn't know her name and he never asked. The conversation was the same every time they met and that was how it was supposed to be.

After lingering at the pet stall for a minute or so Archie moved over to the bag stall and made a point of looking through the range of bags hanging from the sides and top of the unit until an elderly woman got up from the folding chair she had been sat on and spoke to him.

'Can I help you?', asked the grey-haired woman in her sixties. A slight gust of wind caught her loose hair causing her to brush it from her eyes with a hand. Archie looked on as if trying to decide whether she was making some sort of signal. His mind was still a little foggy from the cannabis joint he had smoked for breakfast.

The old woman stood there waiting for a reply. The lad was supposed to stick to the script and any deviation meant she was to retain the bag. She was about to take a seat once more when the youth spoke.

'I need a large carry bag for my clothes. Do you have any?'.

The old woman looked at the young man. She had dealt with him a few times now but today he looked a little out of sorts. He looked stoned. But he had stuck to the script. Her own instructions were clear. If he said the right words, give him the bag. If not, keep it and it will be collected by the same person who dropped it off. Deciding he had passed the test, but only just, she reached under the stall and produced a black canvass holdall and lifted it up onto the table.

'Is this any good to you. It's a tenner'.

'I'll take it', replied Bradshaw.

Archie handed over the twenty pound note he had kept ready in his front pocket, and this was taken from him by the old woman.

The holdall felt heavier than normal, the grip handle biting into his palm a lot more than before. Bradshaw turned to the old woman who was now offering him a ten-pound note. His change. Taking the proffered note Archie placed it straight into his pocket and set off through the crowded market once more.

It was unusually warm for late March as he pushed his way through the crowds heading towards the tube station. Archie entered the underground system making towards the Hammersmith and City Line. On the platform Archie sat on the cold steel bench, the bag between his legs. Taking off his coat he wiped the sweat from his brow with the sleeve of his jumper.

Why was he sweating so much?

Reaching into his pocket he retrieved the ten-pound note. Stapled to the note was a return railway ticket. Its destination was Leicester. Archie had never been to Leicester before and wondered how far away it was from London. Turning over the note he saw written in the top corner the word, 'Shoreditch'. This was next week's meeting point. Shoreditch market.

The train arrived with the usual whoosh of hot air and Archie found a seat in the rear carriage which was only lightly occupied. Archie looked down at the bag, now sat on his lap with his arms around it for protection. Anyone in an official capacity looking at the young man would surely be suspicious. Archie Bradshaw was sweating profusely and held on to the bag for dear life. Watching the train doors open and close at each stop Bradshaw became more and more paranoid, clutching the bag tighter with each stop. Eventually the tube train pulled into St Pancras. Bradshaw, bag in tow, left the train and headed up the escalators towards the fresh air of the mainline railway station.

London St Pancras concourse was not too busy. It was still early, and Bradshaw had over half an hour before he was to board the 14.55 hours train to Nottingham. Still sweating, he walked over to the small refreshment kiosk and asked for a can of coke and some kit-kat chocolate. Bradshaw only had the ten-pound which he had received in change at the market stall earlier and offered it over to the young man behind the counter.

'Two fifty', stated the kiosk attendant to the dodgy looking bloke in front of him.

Bradshaw took his change, pocketed the items and walked over to an empty bench with a view of the large departures board. Missing the train could, no, probably would, cost him his life. He would wait here until it was ready to board.

The can opened with a hiss of gas and a thirsty Archie Bradshaw took a long gulp of the brown liquid. It felt so good. Breaking the chocolate in half he ate the sugar laden brown slab in two mouthfuls before quenching his thirst with the remains of the can.

The man at the barrier removed the stretched tape and gave a blow on his whistle.

'Nottingham train. Boarding platform two', he bellowed out.

Archie picked up the bag and ambled over to the barrier joining an ever-increasing queue of people. Offering his ticket to the ticket collector it was stamped and given back to Archie who walked to the far end of the train as instructed where he once again placed the bag in the luggage rack before taking a seat with a view of the item.

As the whistle sounded Archie Bradshaw started to feel a little more relaxed. He would soon have another good pay day, cash in his pocket, and an ability to buy what he needed. Another dose of 'H' perhaps. Today was another good day for Archie, or so he thought. But Archie Bradshaw's luck was about to run out.

Martin Smith had worked at St Pancras station for a couple of years and had got to know most of the regular travellers. He had served the scruffy bloke in front of him several times now and each and every time this particular scruffy young man left his rubbish behind. It was beginning to piss him off. Just as he was about to walk over and recover the rubbish two BTP, British Transport Police, officers walked up to the kiosk. No doubt after a couple of freebie coffee's thought Martin.

The officers, a male and a female not much older than himself, approached and gave him a nod with the customary, 'How's it going?'.

Martin, still pissed off by the actions of the scruffy bloke gave the officers a few choice words which he regretted straight away.

'Not good. Why don't you go and challenge the scruffy git who's left his litter everywhere and earn yourself a cup of tea guys'.

'Hardly the crime of the century Martin', replied the female officer.

'No, but it is a bloody crime and you're not doing anything else. Give him a ticket or something'.

The officers, sensing they were on a loser and there would be no free tea here today, wandered off. As they walked away Martin called after them.

'Scruffy young bloke, green hooded coat, carrying a big canvas bag'.

The officers looked at each other and with some reluctance walked down the platform along the outside of the train. As they were approaching the last carriage of the train the whistle sounded. Walking along the windows of the last coach the young female officer tapped her colleague on the shoulder.

'There'.

'Where?', replied the skinny male officer watching the train slowly pull away.

'BX from Kilo 27', went the young female officer, her colleague looking on rather clueless.

'Kilo 27 go ahead'.

'Train just leaving St Pancras, Nottingham bound. Male located in rear carriage I believe may be wanted. IC1, Male, 20-25 years, dark jumper, name of Archibald Bradshaw'.

'Kilo 27 stand by'.

As the officers waited on a response from the control room Archie Bradshaw settled into his seat. It was Bedford, Market Harborough, then Leicester. He could relax for half an hour at least.

'Kilo 27 from BX', went the radio attached to the young officer's vest.

'Kilo 27. Go ahead BX'

'Confirmed. Archibald Bradshaw is wanted for Failing to appear at Westminster Magistrates Court and Failing Police Bail. The OIC is a DC Dave Carter, BTP FHQ Robbery Squad'.

Kate Simmons had been in the BTP for nearly two years and was approaching the end of her probationary period. She was keen and ambitious, in contrast to her colleague, a newbie with only five months service and didn't know his arse from his elbow.

Within two minutes of the call from the control room Kate received a separate call on her personal mobile. She listened carefully to the caller and repeated back to him exactly what he had said. Five minutes later she was at the refreshment kiosk once more thanking a stunned Martin for his public spiritedness.

'How did he pay for the refreshments Martin? The scruffy bloke', asked Simmons.

Martin checked the small till. It had been a quiet day so far and he had actually been the last customer to have paid with a note. Taking out the ten pound note he held it up to the female officer.

'He paid with this'

Seizing the note PC Kate Simmons placed it into a plastic property bag which she sealed and signed in the presence of the attendant then proceeded to take an account of the whole incident which she recorded in her pocket notebook and had Martin sign the account. A trip to the railway control centre and a copy of the concourse CCTV was next, again bagged and tagged, then finally a trip to Force Headquarters and the Robbery Squad office to meet up with DC Dave Carter.

As Kate handed over the exhibits to an excited Dave Carter the 14.55 hours service from London St Pancras to Nottingham was arriving at Market Harborough.

Bradshaw watched closely as the train pulled in at Market Harborough. Nothing happened at Bedford, and it looked like it was going to be the same here. But at the last second a leather clad biker wearing a full-face helmet appeared from the carriage in front. The biker was carrying an identical canvas holdall and placed it carefully into the luggage rack before removing its twin, the one Bradshaw had put in situ an hour earlier. Just as the automatic doors were about to close the biker together with the holdall left the train and within seconds Bradshaw found himself heading towards the East Midlands city of Leicester. Half an hour later he left the train in company with the substitute holdall and a half an hour after that he found himself on board the 17.30 service from Leicester heading back towards London. This time Bradshaw repeated the procedure but found that the last carriage was particularly busy on departure and so he had to stand. He placed the holdall into the luggage rack as usual but did unzip the side pocket and remove a number of notes which he placed deep into his front jeans pocket. Payday bonus thought Bradshaw.

The journey was uneventful until the train came into Wellingborough where another leather clad biker boarded, took the canvas bag and once more replaced it with an identical version.

At 19.15 Bradshaw left the train at St Pancras and headed towards the Euston Road exit with a much lighter bag slung over his shoulder. Inside he knew would be a number of rolled up newspapers together with a brown manilla envelope containing £500 cash.

Outside of the main station building is a side street upon which much of the waste recycling for the station ends up. Three large heavy duty steel bins are located on the road, surrounded by portable fencing. Bradshaw knelt and started to rummage through the bag. He would throw the bag into one of the skips once he had found his stash of cash.

It was dark and Archie Bradshaw had only one thing on his mind. His cash. He had not seen the approaching couple until too late. It was just an older geezer with a young girl, probably a pro he had just picked up. Ignoring them, his assessment was all wrong.

One moment he was knelt over the bag, the next he was being dragged face down, a knee pressing into his back, his arms being wrenched from his shoulder blades.

DC Dave Carter didn't need to ask twice. PC Kate Simmons jumped at the chance of a bit of plain clothes work with the experienced detective. After taking the call from Carter the young Police Constable had diligently watched the CCTV to confirm Bradshaw's departure on the 14.55 hours service to Nottingham and placed calls to both the Leicester and Nottingham BTP offices passing his details with a request to stop and arrest anyone matching his description. There had been no joy from this request and following Carter's request she had agreed to take a gamble on Bradshaw's return to the Capital and had lain in wait watching every train arrival from the North.

Carter knew Bradshaw would return to the city. It was his safety zone. He had gone to ground recently but the detective felt sure that he was holed up somewhere in London. He would be coming back, and Carter was going to stay put for as long as it took. Fortunately for Simmons, not fully aware of this aspect of the plan, the wait wasn't too long. As each train arrived at the capital from the North and Midlands its passenger numbers thinned out considerably.

Like most major cities there is an early population influx followed by a late afternoon outflow as workdays of the travelling public conclude. As the 19.15 train from the Midlands arrived it was Simmons who noticed the target at first. Tapping Carter on the elbow she turned away from the much lighter flow of arriving passengers and quietly spoke whilst using a compact to give the impression she was checking her look.

'Got him. Man with bag slung over shoulder walking behind an elderly couple dragging two small blue suitcases'.

Carter, wearing a hooded top under his jacket, pulled up the hoodie to partially cover his face before turning to Simmons and placing his right arm over her shoulder. He gently pulled her in close. Anyone leaving the train and approaching the barrier would only see what appeared to be a couple embracing near the refreshment kiosk with little view of the male's face.

'That's him', whispered Carter.

'Just stay put for a few seconds and pull away when he's passed us', Carter continued into her ear.

Simmons rested her head on his arm and watched. The guy with the bag passed through the barrier and headed off towards the Euston Road exit. Simmons pulled away and both officers headed towards the exit, following at a distance. Carter watched as Bradshaw headed out of the station and not towards the underground as he had expected. As their target took a sharp left down the side street running adjacent to the station all Carter could see up ahead was a row of waste bins. Taking hold of Simmons hand, he once again whispered.

'We are a couple. Wait until we're close then leave him to me'.

Simmons, not happy with his sexist request, just smiled through gritted teeth.

She felt Carter quicken his pace as their target suddenly crouched down up ahead and appeared to be rummaging through the bag. Her first thought was a weapon. Maybe he was going for a gun. They were only five meters away now and he was still pulling things out of the bag. Who knows what he was looking for.

'Fuck this for a laugh', she thought and without waiting for the detective's approval Simmons ran the last few meters and threw herself at her target, grabbing an arm and pulling him fiercely off balance. A split-second later Carter was beside her gripping the other arm, twisting and landing squarely on the back of Archie Bradshaw. Bradshaw landed face down with a thump, all remnants of oxygen quickly leaving both his lungs.

'You, my friend, are nicked'. There was no real struggle from Bradshaw, still struggling to breathe, as Carter went through the official Police caution.

Dragging Archie Bradshaw to a sitting position Carter smiled as he requested his colleague call in the arrest. Looking at Bradshaw, Carter noticed he was not in a good way. In fact he looked like he was back on the gear. Still panting for breath Bradshaw looked to his right and appeared to be concerned about something. He tried to speak but couldn't. Bradshaw just looked to his right again, nodding towards something.

Carter just shook his head.

'Don't worry Archie. You are not going anywhere other than the nick mate. Now let's have a look at this bag'.

Whilst Carter dealt with the bag Simmons removed her Force radio from her small bag and made the call. Neither she nor the detective noticed the approaching motorcycle as they went about their business.

Simmons hit the transmit button.

'BX from…..', but she was unable to complete her communication. She was cut short by the silenced round of a Glock 17 military issue pistol. Simmons was killed instantly, the round entering her head at the base of the skull, blood splatters hitting both Carter and Bradshaw. The second round took out the detective whilst the third and fourth finished of a terrified Archie Bradshaw whose contract was now most definitely terminated.

The assassin would have put a second round into the other two individuals were it not for a second motorbike, now entering the road. Comfortable that the job was done the leather clad assassin sped off on the black Honda 750 taking the Euston Road, quickly disappearing into the city and its darkened streets.

The second biker, also clad in full black leathers slowed at the bloody scene but did not stop. Instead, this second biker also sped off into the city. The following biker had a bad feeling. He didn't want to be associated with any of this and made his way to the Highgate area of London at speed on his own 900 cc Ducati.

Twelve minutes later, Tom pulled up opposite Grace's flat and waited.

Chapter 25

Grace loved the open road.

It was dark but visibility was still good on the back roads heading South. One more job she had been told but deep down she knew they would never leave her alone. She didn't exist. She could be terminated at any time by any number of organisations, and she wouldn't be missed by anyone. Truth was, until Tom appeared she had no one. Sure, she had a few friends she had made in London whilst working for a variety of finance and accountancy firms, but there was no real history to them. She had no mother, no father, both had opted to give her away at an early age. Her adopted parents were kind but had long since departed this world. Before their deaths Grace Canning had been introduced into the murky world of war and espionage. That was their legacy to her.

Speeding along the A10 towards Hertford and then on to Stevenage, Grace recalled her early days and the circumstances that led her to this point. A point where she herself no longer knew who she was. Was she a secretary, a personal assistant, drug courier, or trained assassin working for the government?

Truth was, she didn't know.

She had been hiding for years, trying to change, but however hard she tried, however far she travelled, someone always found her.

Pulling back on the throttle Grace increased her speed. A change of direction saw her briefly retrace her route northwards. After thirty minutes it was time for a surveillance check.

Grace pulled over at the side of the road.

The entrance to the church gave her some protection from a following vehicle. Inside, the graveyard was quiet. The gravestones reflecting the moonlight gave the scene a gothic feel. Memories of her early life appeared inside her head. Her service with the IDF came flooding back. More memories of death whilst serving with the Israeli Defence Force returned. Other graves, but not those covered in soil and green grass. Graves covered over with sand and golden desert dust.

Israel 30 years ago

Young Lucy Cohen ran through the sand at Charles Clore beach, just a short drive from the Florentin district of Tel Aviv. She was being chased by her proud parents, Eli and Mina Cohen. Their prayers had been answered on a visit to the United States where Mina's family originate from, and after years of trying for a child, one was offered up to them for adoption out of the blue. They jumped at the chance and accepted the offer, which came via Mina's father, a high-ranking official in the Carter administration. The only stipulation was that the child would need a new name and must be brought up outside of the USA.

And so, at only five months old, Lucy Cohen was born for the second time. Two days after signing the adoption papers the three of them returned to Israel. A new life for Lucy had begun.

Screaming in delight as the warm sea water splashed her, she suddenly stopped and looked skyward.

'What are those papa?', asked the young child.

'Helicopters my child. They protect us from those who would do us harm'.

The momentary distraction by the Israeli gunships flying overhead in the clear blue sky was soon forgotten as a cunning Eli Cohen took the opportunity to splash his daughter once more. Her high-pitched shriek caused Mrs Cohen to smile as she watched her daughter flee from her pursuing husband.

Lucy's early years, living initially on the kibbutz and latterly in the more affluent Florentin area with her teacher parents, were as normal as you would expect. Excelling at everything the young Lucy Cohen soon attracted plaudits from far and wide. Her academic studies were flawless, top grades in every subject she undertook, paled in comparison to her physical and mental strength. At nine she could outrun girls, and some boys, three years older. At fourteen she won the under sixteen Israeli Judo championship. At sixteen, the now beautiful Lucy Cohen was attracting admirers for reasons other than her athletic or academic prowess. Offered contracts by a number of modelling agencies young Lucy decided to avoid all this unwanted attention with a two-year long trip around the United States with her parents, returning just weeks before she was to be conscripted into the IDF, the Israeli Defence Force.

Once more, Lucy excelled whilst training with the IDF, quickly becoming noticed for her physical abilities, her marksmanship with a wide range of weaponry, and most importantly, her linguistic abilities. With her Israeli parents being fluent in and teachers of modern languages the young Lucy Cohen could speak English, Hebrew, and Arabic fluently and had a good working knowledge of both French and Spanish. Her downfall, if she had one, was her skin and hair colour. Too fair and too pale for any clandestine work without some serious cosmetic work, which would eventually come.

For Lucy however, she was happy to just be a part of the IDF and do her bit for her beloved country, Israel. There were opportunities a plenty for Lucy during her first 12 months, but the routine patrols soon became less and less. Instead of checkpoint control work Lucy found herself in the company of special forces units assisting with translating radio communications whilst other team members completed recon operations. As she neared the end of her conscription period, she was making preparations with her parents for a future career in academia with a Modern Languages degree at Harvard University planned in the fall.

Abed Al-Amir was an experienced Commander with Hamas. It was his decision and his decision alone to send the rockets into Israel that particular day. A cease fire had been provisionally agreed but was disputed by both sides for weeks and Al-Amir had seen enough. His Palestinian brethren had been persecuted for far too long by their

Western backed occupiers. It was time to send a message. The batch of six rockets, sent from Northern Gaza into Israel, struck the outdoor market at precisely the right time. Mass casualties was what Al-Amir was after, and mass casualties was what he achieved.

Everything changed that late summer afternoon for both Lucy Cohen and Abed Al-Amir. Whilst her parents were shopping in the Bat Hadar district of Southern Israel just a few miles north of the Gaza strip, a rocket attack killed fourteen Israeli civilians. Included in the casualty list was Eli and Mina Cohen. Hamas was later to claim responsibility, but this was quickly disputed by its leadership who maintained a rogue element had made the fatal decision.

It mattered not for Lucy or Israel. Their retaliation was swift and ruthless. The Israelis had learned much since the second world war. Never again would their people be treated as they had once been. Anyone who takes an Israeli eye, would lose both of theirs.

Captain Ayub took his promising young soldier to identify her parents after breaking the sad news. As an emotionless Lucy Cohen stood over her lifeless parents in the cold mortuary in central Tel Aviv, she made a promise to herself as much as the cadavers in front of her. That promise was not one of future academic study and a respectable career outside the military world of which she was currently a part. No, the promise young Lucy Cohen made was one of revenge. She would avenge the deaths of her parents, of every Israeli family who had lost a loved one at the hands of those Hamas terrorists.

The following day Lucy Cohen signed up full time with the IDF. Her military prowess had already been noted and the IDF were more than happy to accept her. Within twelve months Lucy Cohen had become the youngest female full-time member of Unit 269, the Sayeret Matkal. An Israeli Special Forces Unit.

As a sniper Sapper Cohen was ruthless. Her kill rate was second to none amongst the recon division of the Sayeret. It would take her five years before any lasting feelings of redemption were felt by Lucy but one early morning in the Nablus region, she found what she had been searching for since looking down at the bodies of her beloved parents in that pungent mortuary five years ago.

Five members of the recon team had been watching a remote part of northern Nablus for a whole week. The vehicle arrived and screeched to a halt. Armed men wearing head coverings alighted and took up a defensive position around the transit van, its rear doors open.

The three graves had been dug for over a week, a drone having picked up the activity, and as Team leader Lucy had set up the recon post in the hope that she would be rewarded with her number one target.

Abed Al-Amir was back in command of a Hamas unit after a period in isolation. A drone attack on the Al-Amir household had allegedly taken out his brother, Walid Al-Amir and this location Lucy suspected was likely to be his final resting place.

As the team of Palestinian gunmen held position three bodies were removed from the back of the vehicle. All were draped in the Palestinian flag. As the three bodies were lowered into the ground a further vehicle sped up and came to a skidding halt behind the transit van. The doors were opened and a further three individuals alighted.

'Stand by', came the command.

Lucy surveyed the scene before her. As the final individual left the car and stood upright, she saw him. The man that killed her parents. Lucy pressed her eye to her scope and held the cross hairs over the middle of his temple. It was hot under the camouflaged sheet she and the other team members had secreted themselves under but in a split second, breathing under control, the heat and tenseness of the situation vanished. She was at one with her rifle. She spoke one more word into her microphone and gently squeezed.

'Fire'.

Five silenced rifles discharged their ammo with complete accuracy. Each of the six Palestinians dropped to the ground, most dying instantly from single head shots. The driver of the car had made a run for it and had to be taken down with a double burst from Lucy after her first targets head had exploded. Five shooters, six targets, all dead.

Chapter 26

London Present Day

Tom walked into the offices of Miles Mackenzie expecting to be greeted by his assistant and lover but for the second day running a new face greeted him.

'You've got me again', smiled the middle-aged woman before continuing.

'She's off sick again and likely to be all week, apparently. I'll be here until Friday sir'.

'Thank you, Jane,', replied a concerned Tom disappearing into his office.

Sitting at his desk Tom picked up the telephone and buzzed through to his temp.

'Jane, do I have much on this morning in my diary?'.

'No sir. You have a meeting with the partners at three this afternoon, but apart from that you have a clear morning'.

'Ok, thanks. I'll be out until one with a new client. Call me on my cell phone if anything urgent comes in'.

'Yes sir. Can I get you a coffee before you go out Mr Ford?'.

But there was no answer forthcoming. Instead, he appeared from his office as Jane held the phone waiting for a reply in something of a rush, leaving his office less than three minutes after arriving.

An hour later Tom was stood inside Gracie's apartment surveying the scene before him. It was just as he had last seen it. Tom had no trouble gaining access. The ground floor neighbour had come to know Tom well, always polite when passing. Tom was good at preparing the way for any future requirement, and today, when the buzzer failed to attract a response from Grace, it was Mrs Thomson on the ground floor who allowed him access through the external door.

'Hello. Mrs Thomson its Tom. I can't get hold of Grace and I've left my briefcase inside. Would you mind letting me in please?'.

'Sure Tom. In you come'.

Walking in Tom was greeted by the head of an elderly lady poking out through her front door.

'Thank you, Mrs T. I think Grace is still asleep'.

'Looking good Mrs Thomson. Lovely dress'.

'Thank you, Tom. You are kind'.

Before the old woman could question him further Tom offered her the shopping bag he had brought with him.

'Mrs T. I brought some of those croissants you like from the deli. Here, take these. I'm in a rush and have to go. See you later perhaps'.

The old woman accepted the bag with grateful thanks and offered a quiet 'Thanks' but the handsome boyfriend of her upstairs neighbour was gone.

Tom knocked at the door and after receiving no verbal response began a one-way conversation that he hoped would give any eavesdropper the impression that he was actually talking to someone inside.

'Grace, It's me Tom'.

A pause then.

'I just need my briefcase. It's in the bedroom I think'.

A pause then.

'Ok, thanks'.

During the one-way conversation Tom removed a bunch of keys from his pocket and within seconds had gained entry to Grace's apartment. He had never before been inside without Grace before and felt guilty about this intrusion. But he was worried and told himself this was the right way to go.

The apartment looked like it always did, organised, clean, homely. Nothing was out of place. Kitchen first. Tom felt he needed to be methodical. Each cupboard, every drawer, the fridge, the freezer, every surface, nothing. The bedroom next, same result. Nothing out of place, nothing hidden, not much in the way of clothing missing from any of Grace's storage. Strangely, all her suitcases and travel bags were still here.

Bathroom, nothing.

Standing in the lounge area Tom looked at the fairly sparse amount of furniture. The TV cupboard, side drawer unit, a tall bookcase full of light reading and travel books. One egg shaped wicker chair dangling from its housing hung in the corner. All were systematically checked by Tom with nothing to show for it.

Was this good news? He didn't know.

Just the sofa bed left. Not the most comfortable of sofa beds, Gracie had covered the cream leather sofa in a variety of cushions and fabric throws. Tom removed each and every one, thoroughly checking each item before placing them in the corner of the small lounge.

Nothing.

A vibration in his pocket caused him to break away from his search. Looking at the incoming call, it was Grace. Pushing the accept button Tom excitedly answered the call. Relief flooding his brain.

'Hey Gracie'.

Tom's initial excitement quickly turned to disappointment and concern. Grace was not feeling well and would be off work for a few days. She would call him soon but preferred to be left alone until she felt herself. She was just going to stay at home in bed and sleep it off.

'Take care of yourself Gracie. Have some of that lemon and honey mixture you like and call me if you need anything'.

The call was terminated just as Tom spoke his last and most important words.

'Grace, I love….'

Tom sat down on the now cushion less sofa bed with a bump feeling somewhat deflated and a little worried.

'I don't know where you are Gracie, but you are not here. I am'.

A metal bar at the back of the sofa was protruding, causing him to flinch. Turning, Tom saw the release bar to convert the sofa into a double bed. Grace had told him she had never used the bed as it was too uncomfortable. Standing, Tom took hold of the bar and pulled. The bed slowly unfolded, and the long metal bar now extended to form part of the bed stand. Looking down at the fully extended bed Tom saw that the matrass had a large square shaped zipper going the whole way around the matrass. Unzipping the matrass fabric Tom stood back and surveyed the scene before him.

'Wow! Who are you, Gracie?'.

Tom was looking at an arsenal. Enough to start a small war.

The bed matrass was full of weapons and a range of hi-tech armaments.

Tom stared at the array of impressive arms and various accessories to complement the lethal equipment. There was a HK417 snipers' rifle, complete with scope. A Heckler and Koch G36 assault rifle, three pistols all with silencers, enough ammunition to invade a small country, plus a lot of cash in a variety of currencies. Tom was impressed. The only other person he knew with anything like this was himself. One space however, was empty. Tom assessed it to be a medium sized pistol with suppressor, probably a Sig. He carefully zipped up the cover and put the sofa back exactly as he had found it.

Mrs Thomson watched as the handsome boyfriend of her upstairs neighbour left the building. She had noted the time he had arrived and worked out that he had been inside for nearly an hour, a long time to look for a briefcase. He was also leaving without it. Very strange thought the old lady. Maybe it wasn't there after all. Leaving her cup of tea, she decided to take a couple of the croissants up to Grace. There were too many for her anyway.

Mrs Tomson took the bag, unlocked her door, and climbed the stairs to the top floor apartment. Knocking on the door she stood back to let Grace see who was calling without first using the external intercom. There was no answer, so she knocked again, harder.

'Grace, it's only me', she called, knocking a third time but still there was no answer.

Feeling a little affronted Mrs Thomson shrugged and said, 'Suit yourself', before returning to her own apartment and her chair in front of the window.

Chapter 27

April 1st

As Mrs Thomson looked out of her front window onto a dull London Road, Grace Canning was staring out of a much smaller window onto an altogether different view.

The flight from Luton to Beziers airport is only a short hop as air travel went and Grace had made the journey many times before. As the plane neared its destination preparing to land Grace looked down at the large empty spaces of Southwest France below, not an entirely different sight to the land where she had been brought up.

More memories of a not-so-distant past returned.

Israel 10 years ago.

Mossad HQ

Lucy Cohen sat calmly in front of the most senior figure Mossad had.

'Miss Cohen. Welcome to the Kidon elite department of Mossad'.

'Thank you, sir,'.

'You are a skilful agent and a rare type of person. We Israelis must always be prepared to pay the ultimate price for our nation. Are you prepared to pay that price?'.

'Yes, I am'.

'Then all we ask from you is your complete loyalty. You have talents that will take you all over the world Miss Cohen. Go now. Your orders await you'.

Lucy Cohen, Mossad Agent, stood, then walked out of the Directors office. Outside the door another woman was waiting, more mature in age.

'Please follow me', she instructed before turning away. Not waiting for an answer from Lucy, she led her down the corridor and into a much larger room. Inside were shelves. Lots of shelves. All filled with boxes of equipment, clothing, weapons, monetary notes. Everything that anyone would need to support a covert operation. In essence, what Lucy was seeing was a quartermaster's store. A department store for spies, Mossad agents.

'Sit, please', instructed the mature woman.

Lucy sat and waited.

'Miss Cohen, this envelope contains your first assignment with Mossad. You will need to follow the instructions inside regarding the target but how you complete the mission is a matter for you'.

'How do I…', Lucy started to question but was cut off immediately.

'Everything you need to know is inside this envelope. Everything Miss Cohen. Feel free to take what you feel you need from this room to help you, but be mindful most agents prefer to travel light. Understand?'.

'Yes', replied Lucy.

The mature woman stood from the other side of the plain desk and left the room.

Lucy was alone. She opened the envelope and placed all the items on the desk in front of her. Looking at the picture attached to a single piece of A4 sized paper she was staring at a middle-aged man whose name rang a bell. She had seen pictures of this man before and knew he was often quoted in the media as an expert on middle eastern politics. A likely cover thought Lucy. Quickly reading the one page of A4 she left the contents on the desk and went in search of what she could find on the shelves of the Mossad store.

An hour later Lucy Cohen left the building, her new shoulder bag slung over her shoulder.

Two hours after leaving Mossad HQ Lucy boarded a passenger plane at Tel Aviv heading for the Egyptian city of Cairo. But Lucy Cohen never arrived in Cairo. An almost identical woman, an American language teacher however, most certainly did.

Lucinda Carter walked into the reception area of the International English School in Central Cairo and offered her letter of employment to the receptionist before being taken through to meet her new head of department, Mr L'eclat, a French national, who had found himself at the behest of both his demanding Egyptian wife and more importantly, the Israeli Mossad.

Lucinda Carter was not the first, and would most likely not be the last, agent L'eclat would help out with a short-term supply teaching position but she was the most beautiful. There was no talk between them, that was the Mossad rule for their community sources whom they paid handsomely, just a tour of the school facilities and a talk about what was expected of the new teacher as far as the school syllabus was concerned. She would be teaching introductory French to 9 and 10 year olds with the possibility of filling in for other language teachers as required on a week-to-week basis. The contract was for three months, and it was made clear to Miss Carter that she was required to work three full days a week, Monday, Wednesday, and Thursday, plus every other Saturday morning to supervise sporting activities. There were some papers to sign, keys to be issued, and staff members to meet. But this could all be done the following day assured her new head of department. They shook hands after the school tour and said their goodbyes.

'Welcome to our school Miss Carter. See you tomorrow, 7.30 am sharp'.

'Yes, see you tomorrow'.

A smiling Mr L'eclat watched the very attractive woman walk out the door and into the warm Cairo sunshine.

Lucy, aka Lucinda Carter, replaced her head scarf and hailed a passing cab. She was dropped off ten minutes later at the Ramsis station transportation hub. From there she made her way to the Ciao Cairo Hotel, a small three-star establishment that would be her home for the next few weeks, or as long as she felt it safe to stay there. Mr Nassr, the hotel manager, was another long-term friend of the organisation. He had been vetted by Mossad many years ago who in turn for his assistance contributed to his many vices and children dotted around the Middle East.

Nassr had been expecting a special guest but had not been told who or when. Just that it would be an American and he was to ask few, if any, questions.

'Passport please', requested the overweight man behind the desk. Sweat marks under his armpits were a sign of just one of his many poor health condition. His shirt bulged tightly, each button fighting against the pull of the cotton fabric. The overhead fan spun but it did little to cool anyone within its vicinity. Even Lucy felt a little overwhelmed by the heat. The temperature inside appeared hotter than the air temperature outside.

Lucy handed the sweating man her passport which he briefly looked at before reaching for a set of keys attached to a small block of wood with the number four printed upon it.

'I keep for you?', asked the sweating Mr Nassr.

Lucy shook her head, reached over, and took the passport back.

'No thank you', she replied before walking towards the stairs assuming her room was on the top floor.

'Okay Miss. Top room, no lift', he replied in broken English.

As she unpacked her small travel case Lucinda Carter put away her few belongings in the rickety wardrobe. There was no sign she had ever been Lucy Cohen amongst her things, nothing. The name she had been given was a close name to her own and done for a purpose. Her first foreign mission needed to go with ease and having problems with her first name was not ideal. Hence Lucy became Lucinda. She did not like the manager. Her initial assessment of him was not favourable. She knew that he was paid by Mossad, and this in itself was a worry for her. He was a traitor to his country and would do anything for money. She would make the appropriate plans. But first she needed to shop.

Leaving only a few items of clothing in her room the American woman that was Lucinda Carter headed back out into the warm Egyptian sunshine. Travelling light was an occupational hazard for most agents but for Lucy Cohen, alias Lucinda Carter, she needed some new clothes and a few ladies' products. There were some things in life that women of any faith could not do without.

The shopping district in Central Cairo was not too far from the University and after making a number of purchases she found herself pulling her new trolley case around the lovely green gardens, unusual for this arid land. Sitting momentarily, Lucy attempted to get her geographic bearings. A tourist map of Cairo was in her hand and a route to her target at the Arab News Agency carefully planned inside her head. Folding the map back up she rose from the bench and headed off once more in search of a room for the night. She was booked into the Ciao Cairo Hotel, but that particular hotel was the last place she intended to sleep in tonight. She needed to do some school prep for tomorrow and get a good night's sleep.

The three-star St George Hotel suited her purpose much better and as she walked up to the reception in this much cleaner, professional looking establishment, she requested a single room for two nights in fluent French. French is widely spoken in Egypt and the sign on the entrance confirmed this. A passport in the name of Elise Bourdain was handed over together with a Visa credit card in the same name.

A couple of minutes later the credit card was returned whilst the passport was retained, a normal practice for most tourists visiting Cairo. Tonight, Elise Bourdain would eat, sleep, and prepare.

Tomorrow, Lucinda Carter would return to her new school and begin work. She would return to the small Ciao Cairo Hotel, spend enough time there to be noticed, check there had been no entry into her room, then return to the St George. She would move on to a different hotel the following day if need be. She had four different passports and could lose herself in the city if this was required.

Lucinda Carter arrived for work early the following day and after a whirlwind introduction to the staff Mr L'eclat apologised but advised her that the usual teacher for the morning class had reported sick and she was the only teacher they had for cover. The class was English Literature for the 11-12 year age group and Lucinda Carter had been thrown to the wolves. Fortunately, this group of wolves were not hungry, at least not for the standard curriculum they had been working on. In the desk drawer she found a copy of 'Lady Chatterley's Lover' and began to read out loud.

The class was mesmerised. Turning the nineteenth century novel into an exploration of human relationships the young teacher found that she not only managed to get the attention of the class but also encouraged a number of discussions over the coming days on love, attraction, betrayal, and the importance of loyalty in any relationship.

As the days turned into weeks Lucinda Carter the teacher and Elise Bourdain the tourist began to become more comfortable with life in Cairo. Carter visited the small Ciao Cairo hotel nearly every day, giving the impression that she was in fact a resident there whilst Bourdain regularly moved from tourist hotel to tourist hotel using either Elise Bourdain or a third identity as was the case with her present establishment, Maria Perez, a Spanish/American journalist.

It only took Lucy a week to identify her target. The reporter was a creature of habit and obviously felt safe in his own backyard. After two weeks she was sure that she could finish the job quickly but a slight blip in his routine made her think again, so another two weeks of watching and waiting were conducted. After four weeks Lucy Cohen, AKA Lucinda Carter, AKA Maria Perez, dressed, put the package into her small knapsack, and set off.

Providing fake news reports on Israeli attacks to his Arab brethren was one thing but providing safe houses to fleeing Hamas killers was another. Israel would not stand for it.

To any onlooker Lucy was just another young woman jogging along the perimeter of the University gardens. But she was not.

Usman Ali Razak left his office at precisely noon. He was most definitely a creature of habit and today he needed to ensure his timekeeping was precise. He was to meet his Hamas controller this afternoon who would no doubt make another request for assistance, which he would gladly give. He believed in the cause. Always had. He had a massage booked with the lovely Anita at six, and a family gathering to attend to at seven to celebrate the arrival of his brother's newest son.

But now it was time for lunch. Food had always been a joy to Usman. Today he was once again going to treat himself to a full seafood platter at the excellent Asmak seafood restaurant just a short walk along Nile Street. But first he would take a twenty-minute walk along the green stretch of ground that housed the University. He was always amazed by how something so green could be cultivated in such an arid part of Egypt. It would also give him an appetite for what was to come.

This was a mistake.

As he walked his usual route along the perimeter of the University gardens he stopped at his favoured bench and sat. It was neither quiet nor busy at this time of day as visitors to the City's green area started to build up. Couples walked and talked of their day, students hurried past on foot carrying books, joggers ambled by, out of breath.

Usman Ali Razak smiled at the young woman. A jogger, obviously struggling this morning, she was sweating and out of breath. She slowed as she approached, stopped, and bent over at the waist breathing hard, trying to catch her breath. There was plenty of room on the bench, so Usman moved himself up to one end and invited the jogger to sit. Standing upright again, hands on hips, the jogger smiled back and said something in Spanish. Usman smiled once more but did not understand what had been said. He knew it was Spanish or Portuguese, but the content was lost.

What Lucy Cohen had actually said to Razak was a question in Spanish to which he had no answer and gave her the go ahead.

'I know who you are. Do you know who I am?', was the question.

Instead of immediately taking up his offer of a seat Lucy began to stretch in front of the open-mouthed Arab, clearly enjoying the spectacle. Using the bench, she did some push ups using the seat before moving on to the side to complete a couple of leg stretches.

Usman watched the show, finding himself become somewhat aroused at the scene in front of him. As the jogger stretched, using the bench as a piece of gym equipment, he thought nothing of the fact that she eventually moved to a position behind him.

Usman felt the slightest stab of pain in his neck and reached up to swat what he believed was an insect bite. Instead of an insect he found the firm hand of the jogger. His brain was telling Usman to move but the liquid flowing into his veins would not allow it. Within three seconds his body was unresponsive to his commands. Within thirty seconds, he was dead. As the female jogger continued on her way it would be hours before anyone thought to try and wake up the man dozing on the bench. Usman missed his lunch that day, his family gathering, and his meeting with his Hamas controller.

Lucy Cohen's first Mossad mission was a success.

Chapter 28

Agde, Southwest France

Present Day

As the aircraft touched down in France, Grace breathed a sigh of relief. The place felt like a second home to her. It was her go to place for rest, relaxation, and to re charge her batteries.

The coastal resort of Cap d'Agde is only a thirty-minute drive from Beziers airport and after a smooth transition through the one-person customs checkpoint in what is little more than a prefabricated shed, Grace collected her hire vehicle, and was soon stood on the balcony of her top floor apartment overlooking the Plage de Rochelongue.

It had been over a year since her last visit, but the place was pretty much as she left it, if a little stale and dusty. But now, she needed rest. Closing the curtains Grace took a long hot shower, went to bed, and slept.

That was yesterday. Today, Grace was refreshed and needed to ensure her retirement funds were still in place. It was a beautiful morning to take a stroll along the river in the French fishing town of Agde. But it was the small branch of a Credit Agricole bank that she walked into a little after 10 am.

It was still early with very few customers at the bank as she approached the teller.

'Bonjour', said Grace.

'Bonjour', came the response from the teller with a question as to how she could help Grace today.

In perfect French Grace advised the teller that she had a gold standard account at the bank, set up in Paris several years previously, and this morning wished to withdraw some cash. She further wished to transfer other funds from a business account held in Jersey into her deposit account.

The teller smiled and set about the task in hand.

An hour later, business completed, Grace sat at a table at La Marina floating restaurant on the river. It was a little early for lunch, so Grace ordered an expresso and Ricard chaser. Taking a sip of the alcoholic aniseed drink she reached into her bag and retrieved her mobile phone. Taking another sip, she felt the liquid burn its way downwards giving her the courage she needed before making the call.

Pushing each button carefully Grace placed the call to the man she was in love with. It was not something she was proud of, lying to him, but it was a necessary evil. One day she hoped she would be able to explain her complicated life to him but now was not that time. As the phone rang her head started to hurt. A headache was starting. She had a lot of headaches recently. In fact, she couldn't remember a time when she didn't.

'Hi Tom', she started, coughing into the phone making an attempt to sound ill.

'I'm not feeling too well Tom. I'm going to need a few days off I think, but I'll call you as soon as I'm feeling better'.

Grace listened to Tom's response, concern in his voice, asking if he could help.

'No, it's fine Tom. I'm at home tucked up in bed. I'm going to sleep it off so please don't come round. Mrs T is here and has sorted me out', she lied.

The call was ended abruptly as Tom told her to take care and have some of her honey and lemon mixture which brought a tear to her eyes.

How did he know about her love of honey and lemon?

Grace was still deep in thought when the waiter interrupted placing the lunch menu down in front of her.

'Merci', replied Grace and without a glance at the menu went on to order in perfect French. The waiter smiled and nodded removing the menu card without making any notes. He remembered this woman and had taken her order many times before.

Grace always ordered the Sardines here. They were so fresh, cooked on a grill that seemed to give them an enhanced smoky flavour. Looking out over the unusually calm waters of the river she watched the birds chase the small boats up ahead looking for any scrap of food they could get. The calm waters seemed to bring out an abundance of vessels this morning, not just the trawlers. Small cruisers, pleasure boats, even the odd canoe could be seen passing by the floating restaurant. Watching the scene, she was lost in thought. It was like looking at a picture but not really seeing what was in front of you.

As the plate of food arrived Grace's mind was elsewhere. A sudden thought caused her to speak up out loud.

'How do you know that?', Grace exclaimed.

'Pardon mademoiselle', responded the waiter.

'Sorry', replied Grace, a confused look upon his face. The waiter stood beside the table unsure as to what was required, if anything, from this strange but fairly regular customer.

'This looks amazing. Thank you'.

The waiter left Grace to her lunch, shrugging his shoulders and muttering to himself as he went.

The dish did actually look and smell great. The oval shaped plate had three large sardines at each end, whilst a small green salad surrounding a small portion of rice occupied the mid-section. The aroma drifted upwards towards her nose and Grace breathed in the smell of the freshly cooked fish.

Oh, how she wished for a simpler life free of the memories of her troubled past. At least she could escape here for a while as she had done many times before, and not always alone.

The dreams had been bothering her a lot recently. She had been to many places in the world and in some of those places she had been happy. Her recollections, however, were vague.

A faceless man accompanied her. Someone she knew was important but a figure she couldn't remember any details of. Why?

Grace devoured the food in front of her, removing the flesh of the small fishes from the bones with surgical precision. It was an art in itself, which all sardine lovers had to perfect to prevent that one devilish bone from intruding into your throat.

As the waiter removed her plate Grace sat back and watched the flow of the river once more. A slight breeze in the air brought with it the noise of people frequenting the daily market a short distance away. France loved its markets and Agde had a reputation for one of the largest outdoor markets in the area. Grace left two twenty euro notes on the table and headed off to take a look at what was on offer today.

Chapter 29

May 1st

St Thomas Hospital, London

Carter opened his eyes very slowly. The light that flooded his vision was painful. Someone was pushing hot pins into his eyes and most definitely didn't want them to open. They had been closed for weeks whilst he had been kept heavily sedated. Carter persevered, and slowly became accustomed to the pain, the sights, and the sounds that began to encroach upon him. It hurt everywhere. His whole body was hurting. Even the slightest head movement caused him to feel nauseous. Someone took hold of his hand. No, not his hand, his wrist.

'Mr Carter. Can you hear me? My name is Alice, I'm a nurse and you are in hospital'.

An attempt to respond was a simple croak. Carter felt as though he was being strangled. He couldn't breathe properly. Something was in his mouth, obstructing his throat.

The voice again, reassuring.

'It's okay Mr Carter. I'm removing the tube now. You'll feel more comfortable and able to breathe on your own shortly. There we go'.

Carter coughed and started to gag as he quickly sucked in the surrounding oxygen. Eyes open now he saw there were two people in the room.

A nurse. He was in hospital. Memories of him finally catching up with his prey, an arrest about to be made, then the approaching motorcyclist. Shots fired.

'Oh shit'.

Carter's eyes welled up and tears started to flow when another voice interrupted. A harder voice, abrupt, cold. A voice he had heard before.

Collins had been visiting the hospital on a daily basis ever since the shooting had taken place. Two dead, Carter the only survivor.

Dragging a chair up alongside the white sheeted bed, Collins looked up at the concerned face of the nurse.

'I'll be gentle'.

'Five minutes only'.

'Sure. I understand. Close the door after you'.

'But..'.

'Close the fucking door'.

The nurse, mouth wide open, had no idea how to respond, so simply stormed out and closed the door behind her as she went in search of the senior on duty doctor to voice her displeasure.

'Carter. Do you remember me?', asked Collins.

'I do', replied the wounded detective, a little concerned at how Collins was invading his personal space. He could smell the mix of tobacco and mint aromas. The tobacco from his clothing, the mint from his breath. Collins had obviously been in the company of other smokers but had not actually sucked any of the smoke into his own lungs himself.

'I need your help DC Carter and more importantly, you need mine'.

Carter listened but made no initial response. Collins went on.

'We think we know who killed your colleague. We are both searching for the same man, and I think you have been holding back. That was a mistake and you have paid a heavy price. Now we need to work together so that we can find this killer. He's a dangerous man detective'.

Carter didn't know for sure and hoped that she wasn't dead. She was just a young cop for Christ's sake. A young girl that put her trust in him. This was confirmation she had been killed. Carter felt sick. He turned towards Collins and retched.

Chapter 30

Marseillan, France

It was the third time this week Grace had visited a market in the small seaside town. She had started off in her most local market in Agde, and whilst there was a lot of choice, she failed to find anything that caught her eye. Cheap clothing, brands she had only ever heard of in this part of the world, stalls full of soap bars, plants, household bric a brac, cheeses galore, everything you could want or need to survive down here. But not what she was looking for. Nevertheless, she spent an enjoyable two hours perusing the wares on offer until her phone caused her to change her plans.

'Bonjour', 'I mean hello, sorry', was how Grace began her conversation with the caller but stopped dead in her tracks as she listened to the voice on the other end.

A man's voice spoke.

It was a voice she had heard before, many years ago. At least it sounded like that voice. A voice that scared her and not many things in this world scared her anymore.

In Arabic the man spoke addressing her by a name she had not heard in a very long time.

'It has been a long time Dark Angel. A very long time. But we have not forgotten you. The net is closing in on you Lucy Cohen'.

Terminating the call Grace quickly made her way out of the bustling crowds of the market, found a side street, and vomited. Memories of a darkened room in the Nablus region of the West Bank flooded her mind. Recollections of a time she wanted to put behind her. Mistakes had been made and she had nearly paid the ultimate price. Keeping the phone on, Grace quickly made her way back to her car and drove up the A9 motorway to the City of Montpellier. Parking the car up at a small Campanile hotel on the edge of the City, Grace paid for two nights in cash then took a cab into the city centre, making a specific request to the cab driver.

Twenty-five minutes later, after two discarded options, she plumped for the third. A small seedy looking back street garage selling second hand cars and motorbikes. It took Grace another hour to find a suitable set of wheels, a 250cc Honda which she paid 1200 euros for in cash, no questions asked. There was no request for any driving documents, no form of identification required, just hard cash and a promise to return and purchase further items should this piece of metal do the job. Taking the keys Grace turned to the old man, still smoking the same cigarette he had in his mouth when she walked in.

'I need a helmet too if you have one suitable'.

The door to the garage suddenly opened behind her and a voice responded, 'That will be another thousand euros lady'.

Grace was looking at the old man but heard the voice and the door close behind her with a turn of the lock.

The old man, who had hardly opened his mouth all the time she had been there now smiled, his yellow teeth painted with years of nicotine abuse.

'Do as he say. If you want to leave in one piece'. The old man now decided to strike up some sort of conversation it would appear.

Grace replied, leaning in and whispering into the old man's ear. The stench of his body odour so strong and musky it was almost overpowering, but Grace was now on high alert.

'I'll kill you first, then him if you don't do as I say'.

The old man wasn't expecting this, and his cigarette dropped from his wide-open mouth.

Grace turned to face the voice which belonged to a younger man, maybe forty years old. Five ten, very overweight, dressed in black leather biker's trousers and black leather vest.

As he took off his full visor helmet Grace noticed he was no more handsome than his older friend. She also noticed the tattoos on his arms one of which was associated with the French Foreign Legion.

'She says she will kill us if we don't do as she says'.

Both men started to laugh but the older man's laughter was cut short by Grace's left elbow impacting with his throat in a short swift movement.

The old man sank to his knees clutching his throat, gasping for breath. Grace did not turn but took one pace to her right. She knew the old man was incapacitated and no longer a threat. She was now preparing for an attack from the younger man. She didn't have long to wait as the overweight biker pounced.

Like all garages there are numerous items available as makeshift weapons and this one was no different. Grace took the step to her right, picked up one of those items, a twelve-inch adjustable spanner. Not the biggest tool in the garage, he was actually on his way towards her, but the one she now held would do the trick.

The problem with anger is it clouds your mind. It makes you less logical. The biker heading toward Grace had initially been filled with greed, seeing a defenceless woman in the garage he ran with his uncle. Now that mind was clouded with even more anger. He had been a Legionnaire it was true, but that was over fifteen years ago. He would crush this woman. As he rushed towards her, his momentum slowed by bike parts and tools discarded everywhere he failed to see her right hand. As he was about to lay hands on the motionless woman, he further failed to see the short strike coming. It was perfectly timed to meet his temple just as he arrived within Grace's personal space. The biker dropped, blackness enveloping him. Not taking any chances Grace struck the biker twice more, on both wrists. The crack of bone clear to hear.

Happy that the biker was at least incapacitated, maybe dead, Grace turned back to the old man.

'Please', begged the old man as Grace approached.

'Look away. I warned you old man'.

And with that Grace struck him across the front of his head and he dropped to the floor. The wound from the strike caused only a small trickle of blood to drip to the floor.

Checking the old man's pulse Grace confirmed he was still alive. Same with the younger biker. He was breathing and would eventually wake up, albeit in a lot of pain. Picking up his helmet she tried it for size. Yes, that will do she thought. Retrieving the cash she had paid for the bike, Grace left six, fifty-euro notes, but kept the rest. That was the approximate value of this bike she considered. They were about to fuck her over in more ways than just the price and would surely have done so had she been anyone else. But she was not anyone else.

She was Grace Canning. She was Lucy Cohen. She was the Dark Angel.

As Grace left the garage, helmet on and visor down, she unlocked the door and retained the keys. The biker guy had already put up the closed sign. Thanks for that, very helpful thought Grace.

Firing up the Honda motorbike Grace and sped out of the city and onto her next port of call.

Marseilles is one of France's largest Cities and it was here that Grace eventually found what she was looking for.

The harbourside flea market was much the same as most other port markets with lots of fresh fish, cheeses, breads of varying sizes and varieties, plus numerous local wine stalls. But it was not the produce she was after it was a particular stallholder. She had been searching for this particular woman for the last few weeks and today was her lucky day. After leaving the garage and the two unconscious chancers Grace had made her way to Marseilles. It had taken her two hours, changing her direction a number of times. Eventually she had arrived. Her first stop was the port and a final resting place for her mobile phone. She found it late afternoon as a small freighter bound for Tangiers was about to pull out of port. Grace had wiped her phone as clean as she could before tossing it to an unsuspecting North African fisherman as the boat pulled away.

'For you my friend', she called as the weathered looking man caught the phone and looked up at the biker chick stood portside. Looking at the small hi tech mobile phone the man smiled up at the biker, now sat astride her machine, and shrugged his shoulders. He pocketed the phone and went back to work. There were nets to repair during the journey to Tangier but already he knew what price he could get for this up market phone at the bazaar.

Celine had not been busy this morning selling only two items so far. An old brass bed warmer to an obvious antique dealer, probably from Paris, at only twenty euros. And a mixed set of kitchen utensils to an elderly couple for just ten euros. The market was busy enough, just not many people buying her wares which consisted mostly of good homewares and a smattering of potential antiques. She noticed the biker from a distance. There was a vaguely familiar look about her and Celine knew she was headed her way. At 42 years old Celine had been in the self-employed business for a number of years now and had had to adapt to market changes since her law enforcement career had quickly come to an end and an enforced stay at one of France's most notorious women's prisons had pushed her into an altogether different life route.

'Bonjour', 'How are you?', asked the biker.

Celine recognised the biker now, had done business with her before, but still she needed to show a little caution.

'I'm good', replied Celine, not taking her eyes off the young leather clad woman.

Grace could sense an element of caution in the stallholder's voice so decided to rummage through what she had on offer, placing a few items to one side.

'I'll take the padlock, plus the screwdriver set if the price is right. How much?'.

Celine looked at Grace.

'Depends. If you want anything else. I might be able to do a better deal'.

Grace nodded, then took out a piece of paper and handed it to Celine.

'I need these items. Can you get them? I need them quickly'.

Celine took a look at the list of items and nodded.

'How much?', asked Grace.

'It's thirty euros for these, and two thousand for the rest. Come back in the morning'.

'I'll pay you three thousand euros for the lot Celine, but I want everything today. Meet me at the internet café on Rue Tangiers at two. Take this, the rest at two. Do not be late'.

Grace placed one thousand euros into Celine's hand which she held for several seconds making eye contact with the woman she had dealt with on two previous occasions.

'Two, no later'.

Celine pulled away.

'Two, now go', mumbled Celine turning away, starting to pack up the stall.

Chapter 31

Eight hundred miles away from the French port of Marseilles a concerned Tom Ford stared trance like, at the falling rain from his office window. It was a wet blustery London morning. Picking up his mobile phone from the small side table next to the visitor's sofa he slumped down with a sigh. He pushed the numbers once more. At least this time there was a ring tone. Holding the phone to his ear Tom listened, recognising the tone to be a non-UK tone. Grace was not in the country.

At least her phone was not.

'Allo', came a sudden response.

'Sorry, who is this?', replied Tom, standing again, concerned. There was no further response so Tom asked again.

'Who is this? Can I speak to Grace?'.

Shit, thought Tom. I shouldn't use her name.

'Allo. My phone. No call please'. The English was broken, the voice foreign.

'Where the fuck…', Tom started but was cut off by whoever had possession of Grace's phone.

'Fuck', cried Tom, a little too loudly.

The door opened and Grace's temporary replacement came rushing in.

'Can I do anything sir? Are you alright?'.

'Yes. It's all good here, erm…'.

'Maisie. It's Maisie sir. I started on Monday'. So many temps. Tom could hardly keep up.

'Yes, sorry Maisie. Look I have to pop out to see a client, but I will be back in a couple of hours. Any calls, just take a message for me ok'.

Maisie nodded and returned to her desk, closing the door as she left.

Tom picked up his suit jacket and was about to head out when his mobile rang. It was an unrecognised number which he would not normally answer but with Grace's phone in somebody else's hands he pushed the green receive button hoping it was Grace.

'Tom'.

The voice on the other end was instantly recognisable.

'Grace, where the hell are you. I've been worried'.

Grace thanked Tom for his concern but said she was still not herself and needed some more time off and asked if that could be accommodated.

'I'm sorry Grace but I know you are not at home. Mrs T let me in. You need to come back to work. I can't keep your job on hold for much longer. It's been weeks'.

Grace's response shocked Tom.

'What? You quit, just like that'.

The call was terminated.

Tom stood, holding his phone to his ear, stunned. Grace had just quit her job. He had no idea where she was, again. Fuck.

Eight hundred miles away Grace was also stood holding her cheap, recently purchased, pay as you go phone to her ear. Tears were welling up in her eyes. Had she just cut the man she loved off from her life? Would he ever forgive her? She hoped so. Her answer came very quickly in the form of a message. She had not cloaked the call and so Tom had sent her a message.

'I love you, Grace. I can help you if you need me to. I have the skills. Trust me'.

Grace read the message over and over again.

He loved her.

Quickly typing her reply she pressed the send button then turned the phone off.

Tom looked at the reply he had just received and was at something of a loss. There was a lot to be positive about, but he still didn't know where she was.

'Tom. I love you too. Don't try and find me, I'll be back soon. Talk then'.

Striding out of the office he briefly stopped at Maisie's desk.

'Change of plan Maisie. Cancel all my appointments for the next couple of days and re arrange everything for next week'.

Before Maisie could say anything, Tom was gone. On his way to find Grace. There was only one place she could be.

Chapter 32

Rue Tangiers, Marseilles, France

Celine walked into the internet café at precisely one minute to two.

It was a warm day outside and she was perspiring just a little too much. The bag she had slung over her shoulder was quite heavy and she had carried it for quite a distance. Whenever Celine delivered this type of package she preferred to keep away from public transport and her own motor car. So many things could go wrong. No, she was happy to walk. At least this way she could simply ditch the bag and its contents anywhere along the route should she need to. Being found in possession of these items would mean a mandatory jail term.

At the small bar area inside the café, she ordered an expresso and one hour's internet access. The young man took the ten euro note and indicated she could use any available computer. There were eight terminals in total set up over four tables. At each table two monitors were sat facing each other but offset and separated by a Perspex screen with the chairs facing at diagonal angles.

The tables all had at least one person online, and two had both terminals in use.

Celine chose the table furthest away from the entrance. It was partly occupied by a female in leathers. Her motorcycle helmet was placed on the vacant seat opposite. Celine walked over, indicated to the seat and said, 'May I sit here?'.

The female biker looked up, apologised and said, 'Yes, please do. Can you pass me the helmet?'.

Celine lifted the helmet and offered it to the biker, who took it from her and placed it on the floor under the table. On the seat was a brown envelope. It had been concealed by the helmet and was quickly retrieved by Celine. Payment for what she was about to hand over.

A coffee was placed in front of Celine by the young man she had paid, and she thanked him. Shortly afterwards the biker sat across from her rose from her seat, picked up her helmet and the canvas bag from under the table and left with no further words spoken. That was just how Celine liked it. Job done.

Grace saw the market stall holder walk into the café. The payment had been left under her helmet on the seat opposite which had put other internet users off until now.

Pleasantries kept to a minimum, Grace apologised for the use of the seat and thanked her for passing over her helmet. Shortly after the seat opposite was taken Grace finished her browsing, logged off, and retrieved her helmet and the heavy bag and quietly left the café. Only the most vigilant would have noticed the biker had not entered with a bag. Unfortunately for Grace, the studious young man at the front who had his head in a textbook making notes was that vigilant individual. He did indeed notice the disparity between Grace's entry and exit. Shortly after Grace left the café, the less than vigilant Celine also left. A more professional individual would have given it more time but as it was, Celine had bills to pay, and, with cash in hand she was off to pay them.

Within ten minutes of Grace entering the busy internet café it was virtually empty. As Celine left the café the studious young man, who was not actually that young, picked up his textbook and bag before he too walked out the now empty café, placing the closed sign upon the door as he left.

The streets were crowded and made it difficult to keep up the chase. Daniel Steerman was an American born Israeli working for Mossad as part of their external communications team. In essence he was part of a team who were assigned to keep an eye of other Mossad agents in the field. Spying on the spies. Unfortunately for Daniel he was a lot less experienced than his target. As he set off in pursuit of Celine, his mission to identify her and ascertain what she had just sold to agent Lucy Cohen, he had no sooner turned off the main Rue Tangiers and onto Rue Madelaine when he found himself being accosted, dragged from behind down an alley which was little more than a cut through to the port.

His legs kicked from behind at the knees he found himself face up against the dirty cobbled wall. Street fighting was never his strong point, but he made a valiant effort to strike and turn. 20,000 volts for even a split second is debilitating. Grace gave the young pretender a good two seconds.

Helping him slump to the ground Grace was happy that at least one of the items she had just purchased was in perfectly good working order.

'Talk', she demanded as the young man regained his senses. This time Grace was sat astride him and held a two-inch punch blade to his throat. One little movement and his main neck artery would be severed, and the young man would be dead within thirty seconds.

'Why are you following?'.

The young man was sweating, clearly not accustomed to this street craft.

'It's my job', he grunted, his eyes fixed on the blade.

'Who are you working for, and don't lie', the blade pushed marginally into his throat.

In perfect Hebrew the young man repeated the oath that all new recruits have to learn when joining any of Israel's Forces, special or otherwise.

'I'm with Mossad, trying to keep an eye on you'.

'Why'.

'We found a cell in Europe. A Hamas cell. All have been taken care of apart from one. A man known as ''The Saviour''. I'm here to help if I can'.

'You can help by giving Ayub a message. I assume he is in charge still'.

'He is'.

'Tell him I quit. I'm out, ok. I've served Israel well, but now I need to leave all this alone'.

'He won't like it'.

'He'll understand. And one other thing'.

'Yes'.

'Get a new job'.

Chapter 33

Carter was still on sick leave but at least he was out of hospital. He had been released last week and was now working with the mysterious Collins trying to track down a man and a woman who in some way were responsible for the death of his colleague, and, for turning his life upside down. Living in a bedsit in Hackney, marriage falling apart, career coming to a close, all he had left was his obsession in catching these two. He knew he was caught up in something much bigger, but he was determined. And if working with that slimeball Collins was what was needed to do, then so be it.

Carter needed some toiletries and basic life support necessities. There was a large Boots chemist in Dalston, and this was where Carter found himself and where he would make something of a breakthrough. He was meeting Collins later that afternoon but for now he needed to stock up. Painkillers, paracetamol, Ibuprofen, some bandages, dressings, shampoo, deodorant. At the counter the assistant put everything through the till and totalled it up.

'That will be sixteen pounds and forty pence please. Can I interest you in any of our half price men's cologne?'.

'Erm, maybe, yes. What do you have that is reasonably cheap?'.

'Well, we have some good offers on Hugo Boss, Calvin Klein, Joe Malone, Lacoste, Tom Ford, Hermes, Jean Paul....'.

'Stop there'.

'Excuse me', the assistant seemed a little affronted by the sharp tone.

'Sorry, I'll take one each of those, those, and those, please'.

Carter's mind had been blurred of late. He had been here before, seen these names, but now he had something of a deja vous moment. The cologne names again. The answer was definitely here. His files had all been re assigned and so this was all he could do to get a start once more and someone owed him a favour.

Carter placed his paper carry bag on the desk in front of the bewildered Intelligence officer.

'Hey Tom, what's going on. Thought you were off sick'.

'I am. But you're not Andy, and I need some help mate'.

The Intelligence officer took a peek into the bag, then looked up from his sitting position. He was in the middle of producing a report on recent incidents of an organised crime gang allegedly moving large amounts of money by train into and out of London.

'Some nice brands in there Dave. Are they stolen?', asked Andy Robinson, the 27-year-old Economics graduate who had drifted into the Met after ditching a promising career in Teaching went belly up.

'All paid for Andy. Receipt is in the bag. Cost me a fortune today and one of them has your name on it'.

'Not sure I'm going to like this'.

'All I'm asking Andy is you run these names through the Intel system for me. It's just a hunch and it's all I've got left. I owe it to.....well, you know'.

'No problem, Dave. I'm on it. I'll do what I can and let you know what I find out, ok'.

Carter placed a hand on the officer's shoulder, thanked him, and left. And was right. He was on sick leave and shouldn't be here. In fact, he should be somewhere else. Taking out his phone he made the call to Collins.

As Carter was leaving Collins a message, the young Intelligence officer placed the bottles of cologne on the desk in front of him.

Hugo Boss, Calvin Klein, Joe Malone, Tom Ford, and Jean Paul Gaultier. Definitely Hugo Boss. That's the one he would go for. But first he had better start running the names through the system. He liked Carter. He was a good detective and he had suffered a lot recently, they all had. The Met had lost one of its own.

Picking up the bottle of Hugo Boss, he started to type.

Collins stepped off the river boat and headed into Greenwich Park. He didn't like being told what to do by some lowly detective, but for now he knew he needed him.

The men he had just left on the boat were not happy and threatening to make life difficult for all parties. Their plan to incorporate crime into their government financial plans was going astray and heads were being called for. Collins biggest worry was that if a scapegoat was needed, he was first on that list. He needed an exit plan. After a lifetime of serving the state, he knew that he was just a number. An expendable number.

'You're late Carter'.

'So, fire me Collins. I'm happy to work alone'. Carter was in a grumpy mood and wasn't going to take any shit from this government spook.

Collins was sat at a table in the small cafeteria inside the Cutty Sark experience. An empty coffee cup in front of him told Carter he had been waiting for some time.

There was an uncomfortable silence between the two men. Collins was staring up at the standing detective. Carter chose to remain standing. Psychologically, he had the upper hand being in an elevated position. Carter remained standing until Collins gestured to the chair.

'Sit'.

Carter ignored the instruction, instead turning and walking away. A concerned Collins sat upright at first fearing the detective was about to leave but watching him stand at the food counter and order a coffee he relaxed once more. Collins had underestimated Carter's abilities. He needed this detective more than he cared to admit. As Carter returned with a coffee, he sat opposite the government man.

'So, tell me Collins. What is it that you do again?'.

'I do whatever the government tell me to do'.

'And the man I am looking for. What does he have to do with you?'.

'Let's just say he is part of a team that have gone rogue. We've been looking for them for some time'.

Carter sipped his coffee, not taking his eyes off Collins.

'Sorry, did you want another coffee. I should have asked', Carter responded sarcastically.

'I did, but no matter. Look, we're not friends, we're not colleagues, we are just hunting the same man. Let's just get on with it'.

'Fine, but I get to arrest this man. Understand?'. Carter paused midway through lifting the cup to his lips, waiting for a confirmatory response from the government man.

'Of course', replied Collins after a pause. He had no intention of letting Carter anywhere near his assets. They needed to be brought in for a full de briefing and assessment. Carter was a means to an end.

Carter took out a small notebook and flipped through a few pages. He didn't trust Collins but knew he was the only way he was going to get his man.

'Ok. I think I found a link to one of the names connected to the man on the CCTV from the underground. He, I believe, is the same man who arrived at London's City Airport and who also came into the UK from Ireland'.

Collins was nodding and leaned in closer.

'And?'.

'The name Hugo Ross struck a bell. I was at a chemist shop and purchased a load of men's cologne. Look at the brand names'.

Collins turned the notebook towards himself and read.

Hugo Boss/Hugo Ross

Joe Malone/Joseph Malone

Calvin Klein/Kelvin Klein

Jean Paul Gaultier/John Paul/Paul Gaultier

Tom Ford/Thomas Ford

'And these names. You have found something?'.

Carter smiled.

'Three of them have been used in England and Wales over the last six months, with pings on ANPR, credit cards, and various local authority searches. It was something I was working on before I got shot and since then I've been out the loop of course'.

'Come on Carter get on with it for fuck sake'.

'Hugo Ross and Joseph Malone are names that have been used. Checks appear to confirm the description of the holders of those names match the description of the man we are looking for'.

'Do we have addresses for them?', asked Collins.

'Nope. The names have simply disappeared off the radar. But'.

'But?', replied Collins, now sat upright again, expecting something positive was about to be unveiled.

'Thomas Ford is a name that has been found on a number of searches and that name is still active. We're struggling to find any visuals, but I have a work and home address on this one name'.

'Then let's go'.

Chapter 34

Cap D'agde, France

Grace plunged into the clear blue water of the Mediterranean and swam out as far as she felt it safe to do so. Treading water, she turned to look back at the beach. The weather was unusually warm for the time of year with temperatures in this part of the French coast reaching record temperatures. Yesterday it reached 27 C on the coast and a record high of 31 C in Avignon. The water was still a little fresh though. It usually took until late June for the sea water to reach a reasonable temperature, so Grace was pleased to get some swim time in. The flippers made it easy to tread water and as she looked back, she saw that the beach was beginning to fill up. Locals and tourists were looking to take advantage of the good weather.

Grace preferred it quiet.

Snorkel inserted into her mouth once more she pulled her face mask back into place and headed back to shore.

Fifteen minutes later Grace was unzipping her wetsuit and taking in a few of the sun's rays as she lay on her towel on the fine sand. To any onlooker she was just another tourist sunbathing on the sand.

As Grace lay upon her towel taking in the sun a male passenger was about to make his way through customs at Marseilles airport. The customs officer accepted the passport and glanced up at the businessman stood before him. The official handed the passport back and said in broken English, 'Welcome to France Mr Malone'.

The man with the Joseph Malone passport thanked the official and headed straight for the Hertz car hire desk.

Chapter 35

Shoreditch, London

Dave Carter sat in the front passenger seat watching the road ahead, and in particular, the side entrance to the small internet café on the end of Willow Street. Collins had insisted on taking his vehicle, not what Carter had expected but nonetheless he still felt uncomfortable in this high spec BMW. Collins sat in the driver's seat looking through the computerised information Carter had arranged to be sent to his personal laptop which he insisted was secure.

After an hour Collins had read enough and closed the laptop down.

'Any movement?'.

'Nothing at all', replied Carter.

'Ok. Time to go'.

Collins placed the laptop under his seat then reached inside his coat and removed a pistol which he cocked and checked. The 'clack click' sound of the pistol being loaded startled carter.

'What the fuck are you doing Collins'.

'Ready?'.

Carter was a little shocked at the sight of the weapon. Collins could see he was shaken up.

'Look, we are after a dangerous man. It's insurance'.

'I thought we would call in some armed response team', said Carter, a worried look on his face.

'I am the armed response. Now come on'.

Collins arrived at the internet café first, followed by a struggling Carter. He was not really up to this, physically but couldn't stop now. Not at this late stage. Collins stopped abruptly before entering and turned to Carter.

'Do you have your warrant card on you?'.

'Of course, why?'.

'You do the talking inside. Do the Cop thing and make something up about the tenant upstairs'.

'Ok. What are you going to do?'.

'I'll hang around here. Keep an eye on the entrance. Don't give too much away Carter'.

Carter ignored that last remark and walked in. He knew what he was doing. Who the hell did Collins think he was?

Carter used his Police skills inside the café whilst Collins made his way up the external stairs to the apartment's front door.

Twenty minutes later Carter appeared at the front door to the apartment. Collins was nowhere to be seen so in true Police fashion Carter gave three short sharp raps on the door. No answer. He was just about to repeat the action when the door opened. Collins was stood there, inside.

'How…'

'Don't ask just get in'.

Carter walked into the small one-bedroom studio style apartment. It was compact, neat, and tidy. The entrance led straight into a recessed area, much like a hallway but very short which itself opened up into a small kitchen. The lounge and dining area all rolled into one.

A window above the kitchen had a view of the road outside but gave no sight to the entrance. The kitchen looked like it had some use, but nothing was left out of place. All the crockery and utensils had been washed and put away. There was some basic food in the cupboards, enough to make a meal without any fresh ingredients. Pasta, rice, stock cubes, herbs, some tomato sauces, and plenty of tinned vegetables. All stacked in neat rows. The refrigerator was stocked full of bottled water, some bottled French beer, and two bottles of Picpoul de Pinet, white wine from the Languedoc region of Southern France. Carter made a note of the French connection and stored it away in his grey matter. Carter, notebook out, made notes as he went. Anything he thought may assist his investigation went into this book.

'What's your first impressions detective?'.

Carter was silent a moment before walking into the bedroom and checking through the wardrobe. The clothes here were again all organised in neat rows although Carter did make a note of the fact that for someone living in a studio bedsit, all the clothing was of very high quality. The labels in the suits, shirts, and casual gear were all high end and well above Carter's pay grade.

The bathroom was cramped and had a small basin, shower, and toilet all in about a one and a half square meter footage. Carter opened a small, mirrored cabinet on the wall and stood back.

'Wow!'.

'What is it Carter'.

'Look'.

Carter was pointing at the open cabinet which was full of nothing but bottles of men's cologne. All the same fragrances that Carter had purchased himself. All were names he had checked, at least variations of names.

'Hugo Boss, Joe Malone, Calvin Klein, and last but not least, Tom bloody Ford'.

Carter's phone buzzed in his pocket, but he ignored it. He was thinking. Collins, on the other hand was getting impatient.

'We know about the names Carter. Anything else you want to impart on me that might actually help me find him?'.

'Yes. One thing I can tell you. This is a bolt hole. He has somewhere else, probably in London'.

Carter was looking at his phone now.

'And another thing'.

'What?', asked Collins.

'A man going by the name of Joseph Malone has just landed at Marseilles airport'.

Collins turned and headed for the door.

'Where are you going?', called Carter.

Collins turned at the door and said, 'Stay here. Find out what you can'.

'Where are you going?'.

'France'.

Chapter 36

Grace checked the items in the bag once more. It was not exactly what she had ordered but she knew Celine had done her best. The Sig pistol and attached suppressor she placed on the table. The magazine had ten rounds and she had a further box of fifty. Grace had asked for two hundred, but she knew that would be a big ask. She hoped for one hundred but fifty would have to do. The taser electric stun gun plus charger worked well. She had already tested it on a less than competent Mossad agent. The agency must be dropping their standards thought Grace if that was all they had. It was worrying. Still, she had told Ayub she was out and was leaving this world behind. She was no longer going to be a pawn in their Political games.

She was done.

Staring at the sea it was a good day for swimming once more. The swim yesterday helped her relax, and she was hoping to go out again today. But first she was expecting someone. Checking her watch, it was 10.30 am. The appointment was at 12.00 mid-day. Time to tidy up. If she was going to sell this beachside apartment, she had better make it look sellable.

Grace started to clean.

Chapter 37

As Grace cleaned her apartment three men were on their way towards her.

Collins left Carter the day before and headed straight to Westminster. There was no need to book any commercial flight, Collins was given a ride at the expense of Her Majesty's Armed Forces in the back of an RAF cargo plane which took off from Brize Norton later that afternoon. The cargo plane, carrying a number of cases of British SA 80 rifles destined for use by French Special Forces, landed at a base North of Avignon where a French Special Forces Helicopter was on hand to give Collins a lift further South. At 9 pm Collins eventually found himself holed up in what was in effect a UK safe house in the French port of Sete. Used by British SAS and SBS teams as a base for their incursions into North Africa, it had everything Collins needed for a short stay in France, especially in terms of weaponry and mobility.

By 7 am the following day Collins was refreshed, fed and watered, and ready to do his duty. The coded access to the mini arsenal in the basement allowed Collins a wide choice of killing tools. He didn't need much and after making his choice he removed a set of keys and left the detached barn conversion and went in search of the high powered 4 x 4 that should fit the keys he had in his hand. The outside of the farm building and attached barn had seen better days but the inside had been converted years ago. The large garage was housed at the rear and was little more than four concrete posts holding up lengths of prefabricated metal. As Collins unlocked the prefab doors to the garage he saw that the place was bigger than it looked and held six vehicles. There were two motorbikes, a scooter, a minibus, sports car, and what he was looking for, a Range Rover.

By 7.30 Collins was on the A9 heading South West following a blip on a hand held machine that told him his target was in the coastal resort of Marseillan.

Tom had risen early. He had arrived in France the previous afternoon and headed straight to the apartment he had visited many times before. However, something deep inside told him to hold back and wait.

Marseillan, a typical French coastal resort, it was not in the St Tropez league, but it was close enough to his final destination and Tom decided to book into a cheap hotel and make a plan.

He knew what being cornered felt like and he knew that Grace must feel she has been cornered in the one place she felt safe. It had taken Tom a long time to find this woman and he didn't want to lose her now. It was early, a little after 8 am and the sun was just rising enough to indicate another sunny may day was on its way.

Tom sat in his own hire vehicle waiting. His contact had said 8.00 am and it was now 8.05. He didn't like it. Just as he was about to fire up the engine a motorcycle carrying a pillion passenger entered the small car park at the rear of the hotel. Tom was unarmed but prepared himself. If need be he would accelerate hard and use the vehicle as a weapon. It was all he had. A medium sized Renault Megane car. Watching the scene in front of him, Tom became more and more anxious. There was no movement with the motorcycle. It just remained in place near to the entrance. Wait, now it was moving in a semi circle preparing to leave. Slowly the motorbike set itself up to make a speedy exit. Tom didn't like this. The pillion passenger got off and turned to face Tom's car. Slowly the biker moved towards the car. They were not holding anything but then, suddenly, a small bag was removed from their shoulder, the biker reaching inside.

'Fuck this', mumbled Tom to himself.

Revving the Megane he was about to release the handbrake as his tyres started to scream when the biker dropped the bag and raised their arms. A visor was pulled up and a scream emerged, 'No. Wait. Tom, it's me'.

Tom slammed on the brakes a split second after their release but even so the vehicle had started and was now only a matter of three or for feet from it's intended target.

The biker, her familiar face now in full view as she removed her helmet, approached the car slowly and opened the passenger door. She took the vacant seat and handed Tom the bag.

'You were going to run me over Tom'.

'Sorry Celine, but you are late, and you always come alone'.

'I had no choice. The feds are onto me. At least I think it's them'.

Nodding that he understood, Tom took a quick look in the bag.

'It's all I could get but it will have to do'.

'Thanks. What else do you know Celine?'.

'Only what I told you on the phone. She's back in the apartment, has been for a couple of weeks but seems worried about something. Look I've got to go. You owe me for this Tom'.

'We've known each other a long time Celine. I'll repay the favour and get the cash to you when I can'.

But there was no reply from the biker. She had already exited the car and was now sat astride the motorbike. With a roar the bike sped off into the early morning French sunshine. Tom didn't know where Celine was heading but he knew where his destination was. He was on his way to rescue the woman he loved.

Chapter

Grace was ready. She knew someone was coming, she just didn't know who that someone was. The fact that she had put the apartment on the market made it easier for anyone who knew the business to find her. But that was part of Grace's plan. She was ready to move on.

The knock on the door was expected. Grace had dressed appropriately.

Tom parked up in the car park and watched. He had been here many times before. It was a sanctuary he and his partner had made for themselves many years before. The top floor apartment overlooked the sea and the beaches of the Mediterranean but from his low lying position all Tom could see was the fence and a lot of green cosmetic vegetation planted along the car park edge to give it a more homely look. Angling the side mirrors to give him some view of the apartment balcony, Tom sat and waited. Most of the apartments were owned by the wealthy Northern French as second homes with only a few used as permanent residencies. At least that was the case when he had last visited. But Grace was different now. It had taken Tom such a long time to find her and despite repeated visits to the apartment she had not shown up here for at least two years. But now, she appeared to be in residence. At least someone was. The shutters on the patio doors that led out onto the balcony were up and the furniture was no longer stacked in the corner. Someone was in the apartment. His dilemma was to wait for Grace to come out. Or just go and knock on the door. A glance in the side mirror gave him some confirmation. Grace suddenly appeared in company with two other people, neither of whom Tom recognised. A middle aged man and woman, they were pointing out to sea and Grace appeared to be having some sort of conversation with them.

Grace checked the weapon was in place and casually walked to the door. A check through the spy hole confirmed what the intercom had told her.

Mr and Mrs Signoret knocked and waited patiently. Grace opened the door and invited the couple in.

'Welcome. Please come in'.

'Thank you', replied Mr Signoret who went on to introduce his wife to Grace who shook hands with both and invited them both onto the balcony.

'A lovely view. Just what we are looking for', said a smiling Mrs Signoret as Grace pointed out a number of landmarks visible from where they were stood. The French couple explained that after working and living in Lyon for most of their lives they felt the time was right to make a move to the coast and indulge their passion for naturism. They had holidayed in the area for many years and now wanted a place of their own close to the naturist beaches the Cap was famous for.

Grace knew all about the naturist beaches nearby and whilst she was not a fan of nudist bathing herself she made out that this was a great choice of location. Showing the couple around the rest of the apartment they appeared very keen and with the price just a touch below their top budget they felt that this was a potential deal that could be done without the need to look further.

As the couple both embraced Grace at the door thanking her for her time they promised to get back to her soon with an offer. Grace nodded and invited them to come back for a second viewing should they be interested and Mr Signoret indicated that would be a definite yes, likely as soon as the next day or two.

Grace closed the door as they left and checked her watch. That seemed to go well, she thought and prepared herself for the next viewing. There were two booked for today. Mr and Mrs Signoret at 9 am and Mr Laconte at 10 am. Switching the coffee machine on

Grace had half hour before the next visit and decided to make herself a drink.

Chapter

Tom wasn't the only one watching the top floor balcony. Collins had arrived only a few minutes after Tom and had noticed the blip was not activated anymore. The target was here, in this area somewhere. The car park was very full, there were a lot of visitors about and Collins needed to be careful.

Leaving the vehicle, he systematically walked through all the rows of parked cars. As he walked through the car park a fortunate thing happened. Moving through the rows of empty vehicles a chance glance up at the apartments made him smile. A group of people appeared on the balcony of what was most likely the penthouse apartment. Two females and a male.

'Gotchya', whispered Collins. Instant recognition. He knew the female operative. She had gone rogue but now he had found her. He would kill both birds with one stone, so to speak. But as Collins mind started to focus on his new female target, this would cost him dearly, as his male target was lurking in the background.

Collins waited in the foyer at the front of the block. There was no concierge here, not that expensive a location but there was an option of either a lift or stairs. There was also a stack of leaflets for visitor attractions and a notice board. In pride of place at the top of the notice board was a 'For Sale' notice for the top floor apartment, number seven. As Collins perused the sale notice a young man in his early twenties appeared and stood alongside Collins. Clearly looking at the sale notice he turned to Collins and asked, 'Are you here to view?'.

'I am', replied Collins.

'Me too', replied the young man.

Collins ignored him and continued to look at the notice board, a plan coming into his head.

'What time is your appointment?', pressed the young man.

'After yours', replied Collins.

There was a 'Ping' and the lift doors opened. Out walked the middle aged couple Collins had seen on the balcony earlier. The young man turned and pressed the intercom button to alert flat number seven of his arrival. Collins listened in from a distance.

'Hello. Its Mr Desparte, Jean Desparte to see the apartment'.

Collins could not hear what was said from the other end but knew what his name would be for the next half hour or so.

A buzzer sounded and the lift doors opened. The young man walked in and was quickly followed by Collins. As the doors started to close the unsuspecting young man turned and was startled at the sight of this swarthy looking man standing in the lift with him.

'Hey, you can't…', was the last words that 28 year old Jean Desparte would utter in this world. Collins reached for his head. Putting his left hand behind the young man's head he used his right hand to grip his chin and twisted. The swiftness of the movement took the young man by surprise. The cracking sound of the vertebrae at the base of the neck was enough to end his life cleanly, and in a matter of only a few seconds.

As the lift doors opened Collins dragged the young man's body into a position where he pushed the dead fingers into the base of the lift door lining so that the doors would refrain from closing and headed towards the door to the apartment.

As he stood in front of number 7 Collins knocked twice and waited.

Grace answered the intercom and said, 'Hello'.

A male voice, older than she expected, introduced himself as her next viewing appointment.

A momentary pause caused Grace to rub the back of her neck, a headache coming on. Pressing the buzzer, she advised the caller to come up to number seven and within sixty seconds there was a knock on her door. As Grace opened the door she flinched at the sight of the man before her. Whilst was taken aback for some reason she hoped that he didn't see her reaction.

'Come in please', said Grace, allowing the man to walk into the apartment. As she closed the door with her back she touched the concealed weapon to give her some comfort. This man just didn't feel right. Had she seen him somewhere before?

'Where would you like to start?', asked Grace, her false smile betraying the internal stress she felt.

'At the beginning please Grace', replied the middle aged man surveying his surroundings.

'Ok, well perhaps the outside balcony', replied Grace and she started to turn towards the patio doors but stopped in her tracks. The man was not following behind. He had actually sat down on her sofa and had made himself comfortable.

'Hey, how did you know my name?'. Grace suddenly realised that she had addressed herself as Mrs Canning to any and all of her potential purchasers and had insisted on it with the agents.

'Come now Grace. Or should I say Lucy. It is Lucy, isn't it?'.

Grace was now on her guard, but a blinding headache was taking hold. The man in front of her had a smirk on his face. He was tapping her coffee table in a random manner. Tap, tap, tap tap!

Tap, tap, tap tap.

Tap, tap, tap tap.

No this was not any random tapping. Memories flooded back into Grace's head. Memories of a darkened place, bruised, beaten, strapped to a chair. A man in a white coat injecting something into her arm whilst a guard tapped away on a table in the corner, tap, tap, tap tap.

'Who the fuck are you?'.

The man had his hands in his coat pockets. Why was he wearing a coat? Grace yelled at him.

'Who the fuck are you?'. Grace had retreated to the small kitchen which overlooked her small lounge and was stood behind the counter. An electric kettle to her left, a wooden knife block to her right. Both available and within reach.

'You know exactly who I am Lucy. I'm not your enemy you know. We are on the same side, but you have been acting a bit strange. I've been looking for you. I want to take you home'.

'I am home'.

Collins was sat on the sofa. A mistake. He knew that now. He somehow needed to get closer to her. The hypodermic was in his hand ready to plunge. But first he needed to get into her head, get closer. But she was a cagey individual. Resourceful, resilient, deadly. His right hand around the hypodermic containing the liquid that would finally put her to sleep, his weaker left hand gripped the small 9mm pistol. He could see she was behind cover now, elevated, had the upper hand. There was nothing for it. He was going to have to fire and hope for a good shot with his weaker hand. Collins moved his left hand slightly but that was enough.

The blade came like a bolt of lightening as Collins saw the glint of steel before feeling the surging pain in his left shoulder.

'Who are you', screamed Grace. The knife block now had one implement missing, the item hosed deep into Collins left shoulder.

Collins was now looking up at the suppressed end of a pistol. Still behind the kitchen counter, Grace now retrieved her concealed weapon and held Collins in her sights.

Collins needed a clear shot and to do that he needed to get her closer. Whispering a response, he feigned more pain than he was actually in trying to lure Grace from behind her cover.

'I'm not going to ask again. Who the fuck do you work for?'.

More mumbling. Grace thought she heard the word 'husband' but couldn't be sure.

'What husband?'.

'Your husband', shouted Collins and with a lunge he attempted to rise up and aim a shot at the woman who had the upper hand here. It was useless.

Grace looked on in horror as two things happened in quick succession.

The man on her sofa, a man she definitely recognised from a dark part of her past, screamed something about being her husband then rose and fired a suppressed shot that was nowhere near her. The hole in her electric kettle was now leaking water as Grace reacted swiftly firing a two shot burst killing Collins quickly. He was dead after the first shot entered his chest and pierced his heart, the second shot simply confirming the death with a clean head shot.

Grace moved tentatively towards the dead man, already making plans.

Sudden movement at the door. A crash, another man arrived throwing himself into the corner. A weapon raised, pointing at the dead man.

Landing on the soft carpet in a kneeling position Grace aimed her weapon at this second assassin.

Last Chapter?

Tom left Marseillan and knew exactly what he had to do.

He was going to come straight out with it and tell Grace everything. As he approached the Cap he felt nervous. Maybe he should have played it differently but after searching for over a year when he finally found her he couldn't risk losing her again.

Parking his vehicle in the car park he noticed the allocated spaces were both taken for apartment seven. The first space was occupied by a vehicle that Tom recognised and had spent many hours driving. The second space was occupied by a 4 x 4 vehicle. It's engine was still warm to touch and Tom felt something hurt deep inside. No need to push the intercom, Tom had his own key and let himself in. The lift appeared out of order so taking the stairs two at a time he was a little out of breath as he reached the second floor and the landing off which apartment seven was accessed. As he walked past the lift he noticed there was a crack in the door. Stopping, Tom bent down and saw a person prone inside. Prising the door open slightly the body of a young man lay inside the small space, his neck twisted at a strange angle. The open mouthed body, staring eyes, shocked at the point of death confirmed to Tom what he had suspected. He should have come over last night.

Two, no three distinct thuds could be heard coming from inside the apartment as he arrived at the door. Not waiting he pushed the door firmly and it gave way. Not locked. Weapon raised Tom ran towards the lounge and rolled coming to a halt in the corner. Pushing himself against the wall, weapon raised towards a male sat motionless on the sofa, Tom was momentarily shocked at the sight.

'Grace. It's me, Tom'.

Grace was breathing very heavily, weapon pointed at Tom. The homely aroma of coffee was mixed with the smell of cordite in the room.

'Why are you here? Have you come to kill me too Tom'.

'Grace, put the gun down. It's me Tom, please'.

'Who are you Tom?'.

Lowering his weapon Tom stood upright.

'I'm someone who knows you very well Grace. I know you are not Grace Canning. Your name is Lucy. You are Lucy Cohen and you've had a difficult few years'.

Grace's head was bursting, the pain almost unbearable.

'How could you know that Tom. Who are you ?'

'I'm your husband Lucy'.

'That's what he said before he tried to kill me'.

'Wait!', cried Tom.

Grace fired.

Epilgogue

Fleury-Merogis Prison, Paris, France-One year later.

The prisoner awoke early. He always did.

It was more noisy than normal last night, but he had become accustomed to sleeping amidst a background of noise. Prison life in France was tough but he had soon shown himself to be able to look after himself.

His focus in this first year was survival. Now he needed a plan. An exit plan. And yesterday he found that plan. She had visited him unexpectedly. Given him his instructions and told him to be ready.

Tom Ford was ready.

Printed in Great Britain
by Amazon

79946408R00102